VANESSA
SCHIERMAN PhD
WITCH

SANDY NATHAN

VANESSA SCHIERMAN, PhD

WITCH

A Collection of Three Bloodsong Novellas

SANDY NATHAN

VILASA
PRESS

Santa Ynez, CA 93460

Interior Design: Penoaks Publishing, http://penoaks.com

First Printing: 2016
Printed in the United States of America

I have never been asked to write a testimonial
for someone as well-known as
Vanessa Schierman PhD.
But perhaps only the top leaders in the financial and science/tech fields
are aware of her accomplishments; she is a very private person.

Rather than laud Dr. Schierman for things that many know,
I would rather voice my profound gratitude on a personal level.
Vanessa Schierman has been my mentor since I arrived in California,
a rough and ready kid from the Midwest with lots of ideas and no prospects.
Vanessa took me under her wing and molded me into what I am today.

Opinions vary on that, I must add, but if you hadn't seen the before,
you can't appreciate the after.

Vanessa continues to be a source of wisdom and guidance, as well as friendship.
She also corrects my grammar and table manners as needed.
Dr. Schierman is a perfectionist in all realms.

I recommend Vanessa Schierman as heartily as I can anyone the planet.
Her natural reticence makes some consider her odd.
You may hear crazy stories about her: don't believe them any more than
you believe the weird stuff people say about me.
Whatever you may hear, Vanessa Schierman is definitely not a witch.

William B. Duane
Founder and CEO, Numenon Incorporated
Fortune #1 Ranked Corporation since 1961

TABLE OF CONTENTS

A Note to the Reader from Vanessa Schierman

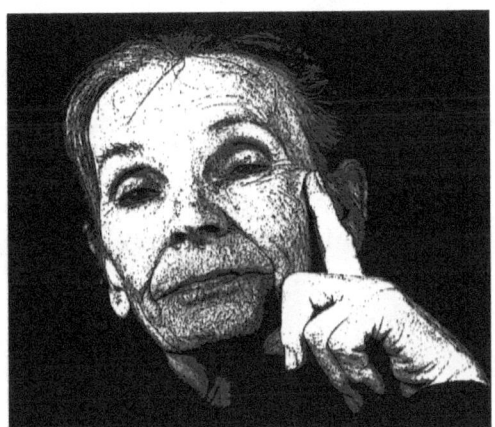

Vanessa Schierman, PhD

If you're reading this, you're lucky. I had no intention of imparting a word of it to anyone. What's written here is none of your business. Assuredly, it is my business. Private business.

Never allow an author into your life. I met a woman, an innocent-looking enough thing until she had me in her clutches. She told me what she did with her time, but it wasn't until I'd opened my heart to her that I realized what it meant. The wretch wrote books. Sandy Nathan is her name.

She tricked me into telling her what follows. Tricked with an appearance of kindness and interest. Pish! I'm writing to discourage you from reading anything of hers. If no one reads her books, maybe she'll stop writing and do something legitimate.

Especially, don't tell her anything about yourself. The next thing she'll do is convince you that you're the most fascinating creature in the world and you should tell her your story.

That's what she did to me, and I told away. But I didn't tell *all* of it.

I can write, too, you know. That PhD behind my name isn't there by chance. I prefer mathematics, but I do know the Queen's English well enough. I could write my own book, if it came to that.

But that's toil and trouble. I allowed that Sandy person to publish these tales. I'm not happy about it, but I have *means* to redress wrongs... Forgive me if I chuckle. (I do hate it when people call my laugh a *cackle*, as though I were a chicken. *That* I am not.)

Well, you've picked up this handful of words somewhere. What have you gotten yourself? Three novellas. Rather generous on my part, I'd say.

Read your stories like good children and don't tell anyone about the content. If this game is fun for everyone, meaning *me*, maybe I'll spit out more. If that happens, this little book will grow. Or not–it's up to you.

—*Vanessa Schierman, PhD*

ΠET WORTH

OUR RICHEST PERSON IN THE WORLD ISSUE:
1997

DR. VANESSA SCHIERMAN
The numbers don't lie: She's been the

RICHEST PERSON ON THE PLANET all along!

ONE

THE RICHEST PERSON IN THE WORLD

THE SCHIERMAN ESTATE, 1997

"I look like *shite*." Vanessa Schierman held the draft version of the *NET WORTH* cover up so that her chief housekeeper, Marjory Naughton could see it. "Can you believe what that dreadful journalist, Percival Palimpsest made me look like? Look at my skin. I look like an alligator, and a ..."

Marjory sighed, shaking her head. "You don't look like that, Vanessa. No one would ever take you for ..."

"A witch. It's been said often enough, 'That crazy Dr. Schierman looks like a witch.' Which is ridiculous. I have nothing to do with brooms or pointed hats. Very few people know about my wand. I'm very discreet in its deployment.

"What am I going to do? I can't allow him to print this."

The cover was glossy black, with *NET WORTH* in its signature font running across the top. Vanessa's head, draped in black, glared maliciously from the page. The rest of the cover said, "Our Richest Person in the World Issue: 1997. Dr. Vanessa Schierman. The numbers don't lie: She's been the RICHEST PERSON ON THE PLANET all along!" The photo caught her *smirking*.

"He used the one where I was telling him about how I was sick of Will Duane being named richest person. If I added up my assets and revealed my corporate holdings, I would have come out on top from the beginning. But I don't flash. I never flash. But I *did* flash with this *NET WORTH* thing, to my detriment.

"What am I going to do, Marjory?"

"I think you are well protected by your use of personal contracts in all your ventures. While *he* has a contract with *NET WORTH Magazine*, as does the photographer, they both have contracts with you that supersede those with their employer.

"The 'first viewing and approval of all elements' clause in their contracts was brilliant. I'd make them do it over."

"I did make them do it over. This is their fifth try. Read the latest article."

Vanessa cocked her head a bit more than its existing slant, listening for a noise coming from the main hallway. She had broken her neck while foxhunting years before. The best medical science could do at the time was keep her alive, with her head leaning forward and to the left. The bones had fused that way. Her appearance added to the perception that she was a witch. "Is that Percival/journalist person still howling?"

"No. I gave him one of your milk drinks. Knocked him out. Doesn't much like his quarters, though."

"I gave that little twit the nicest room in my cellar. What a crybaby. But what can you expect of someone who would dress like that? What kind of professional goes to an important interview wearing a yellow jacket and a *bow tie* printed with *canaries*? I practically fell over when he walked in the living room." Vanessa tightened her mouth and sniffed.

"Oh, Marjory, this is what I get for vanity. For thirty years, everyone has made such a fuss over Will Duane and his wealth. Magazine covers, the television, everywhere. He's a celebrity and known around the globe.

"He was nothing when we met. The son of a garbage collector in Detroit, or Chicago, or one of those places. He had no *couth*, Marjory. Couldn't even order a sandwich properly. I taught him everything, and look what happened?"

Marjory leaned forward. "What happened, Vanessa?"

"He became the richest man in the world, or so everyone calls him. But it's not true. *I* was raised not to *flash* and *flaunt* what I had. So I didn't. But these days, people flaunt every dime.

"But I couldn't stand it anymore, seeing Will everywhere, eclipsing me. Ignoring me.

"Marjory, *I* am the richest person in the world! I always have been. I simply wanted to set things straight with this article. All the brouhaha over his fifty billion. My net worth is far higher."

Marjory's brows went up. She was silent a moment. "Vanessa, I don't like to pry, but what is your net worth?" Marjory asked, looking wary, but expectant.

"Oh, my dear! I would never tell you. You may be my dearest friend and chief housekeeper, but I would never reveal that. It's gauche."

Marjory smiled and nodded, trying to get away from the topic quickly. "It bothers you that Will gets the credit."

"Very much so. I've been extremely restrained in my reaction, but perhaps I had a premonition of what would happen if I 'came out'—I'd have a yowling journalist in my basement.

"Listen to what Percival Palimpsest says in the article." She began to read the draft in its author's simpering, superior tone. She had incarcerated Palimpsest in her cellar rather than let him turn it in.

"The Richest Person in the World 1997"
Percival Palimpsest © 1997 All rights reserved

Not long ago, an attorney showed up at our headquarters in NYC. He claimed to represent a person we'd never heard of. And *she* claimed that she had been the richest person in the world for the last half century. We at *NET WORTH* chuckled politely and pointed to the door.

The *fifth* time the attorney came knocking we listened. Investigating what appeared to be a preposterous claim from a nobody, we discovered that the nobody was somebody indeed. We discovered quite a bit more than the good doctor might have wanted us to. Here's the scoop:

- Vanessa Schierman PhD *was* the richest person in the world and had been for many more than the fifty years she claimed. The head of our legal research department was permitted to examine—without touching, recording, or copying in any way—documents demonstrating the existence of a labyrinth of corporations, foundations, LLCs, and bastardized forms of businesses, not to mention holding corporations and nameless legal entities all over the world. Even a glimpse of these documents showed *NET WORTH* that Dr. S. was the richest of them all.

- She was a real doctor, but not an MD. Dr. Schierman earned her PhD in theoretical physics and mathematics from UC Berkeley, where she was employed as a professor and physicist during the 1930s. Dr. Schierman was among the original developers of the cyclotron,

5

leaving the team when she realized its potential to create nuclear weapons.

- The Schierman fortune originated in southeastern Germany, about the eighth century, when Baron Heinrich von Schierman forced neighboring fiefdoms to form the first major German state. He held his kingdom together by brute force, amassing a vast fortune. Magic was named as a factor in his rise and the continuation of his line. The German Schiermans were reputed to be witches and warlocks from the get-go.

- A branch of the Schierman family migrated to the United States about 1870. They obtained vast land holdings originally reaching from the San Francisco Bay, where Redwood City stands now, over the Coastal Range to the Pacific Ocean. Over time, these holdings have been reduced to a huge estate in Woodside, California, at the top of Skyline Boulevard. The first Schierman to settle in California, "Mad Ludwig" Schierman was the most notorious and perhaps most criminal of the robber barons. He was a contemporary of the California legends: the Stanfords, Crockers, Floods, and Fleishackers. He was richer than all of them, and weirder.

- "Mad Ludwig" was the real thing—mad as a hatter or two. The predilection for eccentricity seemed to have traveled through the gene pool. I interviewed Dr. Schierman at her "home"—anyone who felt at home in that creepy mansion qualified as a hatter herself. I was blindfolded when I was taken to the estate. The good doctor didn't tell us much about the place, other than it was about five thousand acres. *NET WORTH* investigated public records and found that parcels that large are rare on Skyline Boulevard. There's *one*. That property carried an active permit for a top-security mental hospital. Dr. Schierman said nothing about it.

This information is available in the public records. We at *NET WORTH* pride ourselves on deep investigative reporting. "If it's there, we'll find it," is our motto. We pressed for a more personal view of the woman who indeed did appear to be the richest in the world. She put us off, and off, almost as many times as we put off her attorneys.

Tired of our hostess' reticence to "spill the beans," we pulled an end run and had lunch with Louie Schierman, Dr. Schierman's oldest son and heir. Mr. Schierman revealed a lot about his secretive mother and the Schierman family. As his driver waited in his Bentley outside a popular Woodside bistro, Louie regaled this writer with tales in the spooky Schierman mansion on the top of Skyline Boulevard.

"My brothers and sisters have to stay in the hospital. Mommy says most families could use a private mental hospital; we're just lucky enough to have one. I don't have to stay in the clinic because I'm not 'loony' anymore, that's Mommy's word, after Dr. Rudy changed my meds. I'm not dangerous, either."

I asked what the most significant contribution the younger Schierman had made to the world, he replied with great enthusiasm. "The Woodside Rangers. Together with some of my friends, mature chaps like me, with means. We save damsels in distress." Oh? "Yes. We sit in our cars outside the local bars when they close. If any ladies in need of help come out, we take them home."

Louie provided other tantalizing information about the 1997 richest person in the world:

- She's not a witch. People say she is, but she's not.
- She doesn't have a time machine. It's a cyclotron.
- She's not crazy, though some of my family members are.
- The carvings on the walls of the mansion don't really move. That's from my meds.

So, dear readers, truth is often stranger than fiction. That's the truth about our Richest Person in the World 1997.

Percival Palimpsest
Editor-at-large
Exclusive to *NET WORTH*

"Oh, my goodness, Vanessa! That's terrible. You can't let him print that."

"Don't worry; I most certainly will not. But I don't know exactly what I *will* do. Marjory, I'm going to spend some time with the cats. It's the only thing that will clear my mind.

"If *NET WORTH'S* attorney calls, tell him that Percival is out on my yacht. I don't know when he'll be back."

"Vanessa, dear, you don't have a yacht."

"Oh. Would you get on the phone, Marjory, and call that nice yacht man? Buy me a big one. And Marjory, you know I love you, but don't call me 'dear.'"

"Oh, Scottie, what am I to do? I can't keep him in the cellar forever." Vanessa sat on an ornate, cast-concrete garden settee just outside the barn. A dozen cats, all black, gathered around her, looking at her intently as though following her every word. Her favorite, Scottie rubbed against her legs and meowed in sympathy. She picked him up.

"You understand why I wanted that story, darling, don't you? You are my best friend. I can tell you anything and you never blab. Of course, you *can't* blab.

"Oh, Scottie, I've had the most dreadful crush on Will Duane ever since I met him in the 1950s. He was a brilliant Stanford student and I was ... what I am. He was *so* handsome—tall and blond haired. With wide shoulders and that beautiful face. And all that intelligence.

"I quite ... what do they say, *flipped* for him. *Me*, big, ugly Vanessa Schierman that everyone thinks is a witch. I am a witch, of course. But I have a heart.

"He was my protégé in the old days. He had money back then; his father was a garbage collector or something. Will was loaded, but not with couth. He couldn't get into a decent coffee shop. I gave him a makeover and introduced him to the right people.

"Voila! His corporation took off and he's been the richest man in the world since. Not to mention the best looking.

"But he wasn't the richest, Scottie. I have more than Will and always have. It galled me to see him on all those magazine covers, beaming away. Gorgeous hunk that he was. He still is, with shining white hair and that beautiful body. Paying no attention to me.

"Affairs of the heart are so embarrassing. They expose one so and open one to such painful yearnings. I've pined for him, my dear Scottie. And he loves me, as a dear friend who taught him the proper use of silverware for any social situation. And how to answer formal invitations. Don't you see why I *had* to do *something?*"

The cat looked at her, tilting his head from one side to the other, as though he understood everything.

"I thought if just once, the world could know of my wealth and power, maybe Will would look at me as something other than a dear great-aunt." She stroked the cat softly. "The heart never looks at age or impossibility, darling. It just knows when it's smitten, and it doesn't have any choice over that. My crush has never diminished.

"He's still tall and gorgeous; he just has white hair and fifty billion dollars. And I am tall and ugly and stooped, with more than fifty billion dollars. So I'm stuck. Will would think me a foolish old crone if he knew why I want to steal his title — just to have him *notice* me.

"My children would be devastated if they knew what that Percival person wants to reveal about them. He doesn't seem to care how hurtful exposing Louie and my other offspring would be. Or how much it would hurt me. He just wants his scoop.

"I can't let him print that story. And I can't keep him on my milk drinks for the rest of his life, though that is a viable possibility; they are harmless.

"The worst thing he did was contact Louie. I never should have gotten Louie that cell phone. But he is stable now, and he's an adult. What a slimy ...

"Louie *loves* the Woodside Rangers. He and his old fart friends tootle around in their Bentleys with their chauffeurs, pretending to be Don Quixote. That asshole," Vanessa didn't swear, but she relished calling that

Palimpsest creature what he was, "made them sound like they were lechers looking for drunken women to use. That's ridiculous. Not one of the Rangers has had even an imaginary erection in ten years. They're like children."

Scottie stood up on his hind legs and balanced with his front paws on her blouse with its pleated formal bodice. His face registered his mistress' distress. A tiny whimper escaped him.

"That Percival person has no compassion. I watched my children, one by one, all five of them, develop the most horrible mental diseases, with no cure and not much known-about treatment. It was *terrible*.

"I built the hospital on the estate because I *would not allow* them to be given mediocre treatment in other places. They can't get care like they get here, anywhere in the world. And I help other people like them. I treat patients from everywhere in my little clinic. I don't charge them anything.

"Heaven knows, their families have been bankrupted because the medical system doesn't pay for mental illnesses. They suffer so, or they do until I get them expert treatment. I'm not going to expose them to the world. I'm not going to let the world do to them what it did to me."

Terribly tall, even after the riding accident that had given her the strange posture, Vanessa never had any illusions about succeeding with her appearance. She never was a beauty and now she looked startlingly bizarre.

The accident also had gifted her with flashbacks that could come whenever *anything* reminded her of the crash. The sound of a horse galloping. A swaying motion. The crash of splintering wood. She seldom left the estate for fear of one overcoming her in public.

Vanessa had succeeded through her intellect and her will. She had enough intelligence to split atoms, and she had. Mostly, her ferocious love for her family and the people of the estate kept her going.

She and her husband had loved each other. That was enough for a lifetime. They dallied in their marriage bed, making wonderful, flawed children. Until his depression got him and he killed himself. Her family didn't possess a single funny secret.

That dreadful Percival Palimpsest wrote as though they were a joke, she thought.

Vanessa pulled a black hankie trimmed with the finest lace from the cuff of her long sleeve. She wore her signature black, high-necked dress. Ornate black braid trimmed its collar and ran down the garment's buttoned front, all the way to its hem, which sat an inch above her boots. She always wore sensible lace-up boots. No one told her she had terrible fashion sense; she knew it. Vanessa simply saw no need for clothing in any color but black. Or anything but dresses that covered her throat to ankles. Naked, she looked like a very tall bag of potatoes. Why display her form?

"What do you think I should do, darlings?" she said to the cats. They sat in a circle around her, tilting their heads from one side to the other, listening and talking to her in their private, shared language.

She listened. "No. I don't think turning him loose and letting the dogs play with him is a good idea. I need a new approach, a new spin on my story and new pictures. A spin-doctor."

Vanessa thought. *Who could put a pretty face on anything? Make lies seem like truth, and look beautiful doing it?*

Will Duane. Vanessa frowned. There he was, always present in her thoughts. She blushed. *What a foolish old woman I am. All this trouble is because I can't get over my feelings for him.*

Vanessa's pale skin reddened with multifold embarrassment. At having acknowledged her infatuation for Will even to herself. At having gotten this insane *NET WORTH* thing started. At incarcerating the Palimpsest creature in her cellar. She felt so vulnerable, so exposed. So out of control.

Only a person who had felt such tender feelings for a totally inappropriate person would know how she felt. *That ought to include most of the human race,* she thought. But still, there they sat, like Limburger cheese in a bed of rose petals. Like the cheese, the feelings never went away.

She needed a new article and photos. Something to present her in a favorable light.

She needed a makeover of the sort she'd given Will when he got to the San Francisco Bay Area. *Who can I get to do the job?*

Jon Walker. The answer was as obvious as her feelings for Will Duane. Except … everything. She and Jon had a history almost as long as hers with Will.

Jon was Will's private chef—she'd met him at one of Will's parties years before. Jon was never meant to be a cook, even for Will Duane. His brilliance couldn't be contained by a kitchen, even Will's.

She had a premonition that Jon's couple of bestselling cookbooks and the guest spot he held on a local TV cooking show were going to result in a very public life for the young man. She could see the future better than most, possessing, not a crystal ball, but something *better…* that the beautiful Jon was going to be a celebrity and romantic idol to the world's gay population.

Would Jon help her? Probably. She'd helped him get his cookbooks published.

"Jon, darling, it's Vanessa. I need your assistance. It's an emergency. I know you're terribly busy, but… I'm coming out."

"*You're gay, Vanessa?*" Shock ricocheted through Jon Walker's voice.

"No, dear, *you* are. *I'm* coming out." He was silent. "Coming out of a life of hiding to be the person I really am. That's what coming out means. I need your help."

She told him about Percival Palimpsest's terrible article for *NET WORTH* and the photo his man had taken of her. She did not reveal that Palimpsest was confined in her cellar.

"I need a new cover, Jon. Something at least a little flattering. And an article to replace what Palimpsest wrote. I've got to get something soon. The publication deadline is approaching."

"I'm not a makeup artist."

"I know. You have a TV show. But you're the best looking, most stylish person I know. And you have all those makeup people around you, and set designers. People who know how to do clothes. Hairdressers.

And photographers. Couldn't I just dash in after your show and let them have at me?" He was silent. She could feel him make up his mind.

"Oh, Vanessa. I never could say no to you. Let me look at my schedule." Jon was silent a moment. "Tomorrow around noon. My TV program tapes at 6 p.m., but we should have time to slip you in."

"Oh, wonderful! One more little favor."

"What, Vanessa?" Jon was trying to sound stern, but he couldn't with her. They had too much history and loved each other too much.

"Can we do it on my yacht? I just got it today. I got it because rich people always have yachts. It's the sort of thing the richest person in the world would have. And be photographed on."

"Where is it?"

"Sausalito."

"*Sausalito?* That's an hour from San Francisco without traffic." She silently begged him. "OK, *Dr.* Schierman. For you, and only you. I'll meet you at the Sausalito pier at noon, with a full crew."

Vanessa had forgotten how long it had been since she left the estate. Even though her car's windows were tinted as dark as the law allowed, the world seemed to shimmy and expand through the windows. San Francisco was *enormous,* much larger than she remembered. All those new high buildings. Obviously, the new crop of architects didn't remember what happened in 1906.

The Golden Gate Bridge was as she remembered it, and Sausalito was the same. Lots of tourists and cutesy, low buildings where they sold crap.

Driver piloted her Bentley to the dock effortlessly. A preternaturally happy man in a pale linen suit stood at the entrance, holding a folder. The yacht man, undoubtedly, ecstatic at making a sale.

"Well, Marjory, let's face the tiger." It had been so long since Vanessa had left the confines of her property on Skyline that she felt a little queasy at the thought. She brought Marjory Naughton along for support.

"Show it to me," she said. The yacht man jumped. Vanessa always forgot how her voice sounded. Like rasping sandpaper, she'd overheard someone say. She forgot how she looked, too. "Which one is it? The really big one over there?" She pointed at a monster at the end of the berths. That would be appropriate.

"No, that belongs to Will Duane."

Her back went up. "Well, show me the tugboat you want me to buy."

The yacht was lovely, just lovely. Tasteful and beautiful, all slicked with shellac and spotlessly clean. Much more elegant than Will's barge.

"Belonged to a sheik," said the yacht man, studying the contract. "His name's right here. I can't pronounce it."

She looked at the paper, reading the Arabic easily. "Why is he selling it? Did it sink or something?"

"No." Yacht man chuckled. "He gets seasick."

She laughed merrily. That had never occurred to her. She'd never been to sea.

"Does it come with a driver?"

"Yes. And a crew. Abdul is onboard."

Her brows knit again, "Abdul? I thought yachtsmen were all named Gianni or Carlo."

"No, this one is Abdul. He worked for the sheik."

Vanessa looked at the lines of the beautiful yacht from the central walkway of the pier. So graceful and elegant. Oh, she loved it. She had to have it. Perhaps they could move it to the estate and away from the water.

She hadn't thought about the bay or water at all when she decided she wanted a yacht. The image of her in a yachting cap motoring under the Golden Gate came up when she thought about buying a boat. The actuality was quite different.

If she were going to go out on the yacht, she would have to navigate a nasty ramp. It moved quite randomly and excessively. It did have railings on each side. Marjory and the yacht man "mother-henned" her down the ramp, Marjory holding her elbow and clucking officiously.

"Are you sure you want to do this, Vanessa?"

"Absolutely, Marjory. Never more sure of anything." *Can I get seasick before the boat starts moving?* she thought.

Abdul looked at her questioningly. She looked back at him with a hauteur that only she could project. "Well, my good man, do you speak English?" she said.

"Yes, madam."

"Good. My Arabic is rusty." She put a little Power in her smile. She was a witch; the rumors were quite true. Abdul might not have heard them yet, but she might as well introduce him to the person that all of her servants knew and loved. *You are in my power, dear man. Now don't sink this boat with me on it.*

One hard look and Abdul cowered obligingly. She could feel that he was as absolutely loyal to her as the rest of her staff. Vanessa smiled. Being a witch was useful.

"Well, my dear fellow. We'll shove off in just a moment. I'm waiting for my camera crew."

"Where would madam like to go?" Abdul rubbed his hands together, looking up into her face.

"Somewhere atmospheric. How about over there, where the Golden Gate will show in the background?" She pointed at the bridge, which appeared incredibly close. It was a bright, sunny day, unusual for the coast. She didn't want her photoshoot spoiled by the fog, so she'd taken care of that little problem in advance.

"Jon, darling, you're *here*." Jon roared up in a flashy sports car. A van disgorged very stylish people, men and women, bearing lights and small suitcases.

Jon glided along the walkway to the yacht, the only way to describe the way he walked. Jon Walker was more graceful than any human being in existence. He approached her cats in elegance and panache. Jon wore khaki slacks and a blue shirt with a polo player on it; except this player was flying off the horse. His hair was perfectly cut, blond-streaked and tousled from the convertible. Her heart ached when she saw him.

"Darling, can you do anything with me?" She held her arms out, displaying that day's funereal black dress.

"You are going to look so beautiful. Don't worry." He hugged her and kissed her cheek.

We're quite a couple, she thought, *the beautiful television food king and the old crone.*

"I'll trust you, darling. How do you do, everyone?" She waved at the crew making its way up the ramp. "I'm so happy you've come. I do hope you can make me look lovely. Or if not that, presentable."

They stopped and stared at her, eyes widening, brows raising. Six of them, one with a rack of clothes, the others with cameras and things.

"I broke my neck when my horse fell. That is why I look like this." That was more than she usually said about herself, but she had to get them onboard, in every way. "Do we do the makeup now, or when we go out on the water?" Vanessa felt more and more uncomfortable. Something about ... *something.*

"*Let's* do the makeup and styling now. We can shoot while the yacht's moving." Jon took charge. Mr. Style. Mr. Assertiveness. She smiled at him, fawning. *To think that he was 'just' Will Duane's chef.*

"Oh, I didn't know I could look like this. You've made me *beautiful.*" The stylist had washed and blown dry her fine, thin hair, turning it into something that looked like *hair,* not the limp vegetative threads that wrapped corn.

William, the makeup person, made her skin glow and her wrinkles disappear into the luminosity. They brought a kimono-style coat, a rich burgundy that fit over her black dress. Finally, the team wrapped her neck with a stiff, silk scarf. It hid the way her head set on her shoulders.

"Thank you so much. Oh, dear."

"Don't cry, Vanessa; it spoils the makeup," Jon put his arm around her and kissed her cheek. "I always knew you were lovely," he whispered.

"Let's get this show on the road. I've got my own show to tape at six!" Jon took over. Abdul and his crew stared at him, apparently trying to remember where they had seen him. "Go on! Shoo! Shoo! Get out into the bay. We need to take photos."

The movement of the water under the boat was most alarming. She didn't expect it to be like that, chopping and bouncing. Slithering in a distressing manner.

"Abdul! What's the matter?! Why is the deck so—active?"

"It is the bay, Your Highness ..."

"No, Dr. Schierman, not Your Highness. Can you make it stop? I don't like it at all." The closer to the Golden Gate Bridge they got, the higher the chop.

"Oh, no, madam, it will only get worse when we go out of the bay into the ocean."

"Abdul! *Never* go into the ocean! I forbid it!" Vanessa felt most unwell. The moving from side to side and back to front. The brilliant sun. She'd made it *too* bright that day. It reminded her of something. Her uneasiness rose with the movement of the water. That terrible sun fell on everything.

They were settling into a good position for the photographer to begin taking pictures when an idiotic tourist swept in front of the yacht, quite out of control. In a sailboat. What a stupid thing.

If you were going to take your life into your hands by going out in extremely deep, shark-infested waters like the San Francisco Bay, you should have a solid engine propelling you. Like this yacht, Vanessa thought.

The sailboat flew back in the other direction, the long pole at the bottom of the sail swinging wildly. It whipped, and caught the yacht square on the bow. First a terrible ripping, then a grinding noise and the yacht crunched. Or rather, the sailboat crunched. Abdul shouted in Arabic and people dashed about. The photographer put his camera away.

Another horrible wrench and sound of wood splintering. The yacht broke free and the sailboat ... she didn't know what happened then.

17

She was on her back on the deck screaming. The sun shone down with hideous maliciousness and she heard it again, the jump standards breaking. The sound of her horse striking the stone wall beneath the poles. The sound of his beautiful neck snapping as he hit the stone.

Something struck her in the neck and shoulder, something huge. She flew through the air and landed. Somewhere. Everything was quiet, but she heard screaming. Someone was screaming. Her horse. Rhumba, wonderful Rhumba, beautiful Rhumba lay still on the ground. The blue sky. Obscene blue sky. Oh, my God! Her horse was dead.

"Help me, help me," she screamed over and over. "I can't feel my legs. I can't feel anything. Help me."

"Vanessa, it's Jon." Far away, she sensed someone bending over her. He was saying something. "You're having a flashback. You're remembering the accident. It's me. Vanessa."

"Oh, Jon, they have to fix me. I can't feel my legs. I can hear them talking. They're saying I might die. I can't die, Jon. The children. *Who will take care of my children?* Oh, Jon, help me. Don't let me die.

"You're not going to die, Vanessa," Jon said. "It's a flashback."

"But it's so real." She wanted to sob and cry. Maybe she did. "And Rhumba died. And my husband died. He killed himself. Oh, Jon."

"Shh. Shh. Shh." Jon leaned over her. "They're memories, darling. They feel very real. They are real. Your body is releasing memories that it's held all this time. The fear. And terror."

"I can't feel anything." She grabbed at him.

"But you can, Vanessa, you just grabbed my arm. If you couldn't feel anything, if your neck was broken, you couldn't do that. I'm going to ask you to do some things. You do them. OK. Wiggle your toes. Guys, take off her boots." The crew did, watching Jon as though he was a wizard. "Toes work. Let's try feet." He went through her body that way, making sure all the parts worked. "See, Vanessa. You're fine. It was a flashback; awful, but you're all right."

She sat up, amazed at what he had done. "A flashback. Oh, Jon, you saved me." She patted her body, checking that it really worked. "I'm all right. Thank you, my dear."

Jon coughed. "I've got to get back to the city. My show's taping at six."

"Oh, no. We didn't get any pictures or an article or anything. I'm a mess." Her old face crinkled.

"Don't cry, Vanessa. Let me think. You go back to the station with the crew. They'll fix you up in the van. Can I get an exclusive interview with you on the show, tonight? A prequel to the new *NET WORTH* article?"

Vanessa grinned. "You're scooping that obnoxious Percival Palimpsest!"

"If you'll let me." Jon smiled. "I've met him, too. He's terrible. Wherever you've got him is too good for him."

"My attorney will meet us at the station. I have personal contracts for all my doings."

"I know, Vanessa."

He knew her very well.

"You look lovely, Vanessa. Absolutely beautiful." Later that evening, she and Marjory watched a recording of the show from the big TV in the estate's family room.

"I don't know about that, Marjory, but at least I don't look like a witch with an alligator-skin face."

"Seeing it on the screen is so different than watching from backstage," Marjory said. "Though being backstage was exciting, too. I never imagined such a world. Driver and I brought your car to the station. You were already 'done' when we got there."

"It was like magic. They whisked me over the bridge, into the studio and onto Jon's set, just like that." She snapped her fingers. "Jon's styling people put a beautiful bright pink scarf around my head and shoulders, like a shawl. It was stiff material, silk with gold, and hid my neck. Jon asked just the right questions. Let's listen," she started the video tape and the screen lit up.

She and Jon sat in a cozy TV set borrowed from one of the station's other shows. He had dispensed with a desk that separated him from his guests and spoke to her from a lounge chair pulled up kitty-corner to hers. A view of the San Francisco skyline through big artificial windows composed the backdrop. The auditorium in front of the stage was filled Jon's cooking fans.

"Well, Dr. Schierman, I've heard strange tales of you and your estate. Is it true that you have a nuclear reactor?" Jon's hair gleamed and he smiled like an angel.

"Oh, no. What silly bosh. I haven't done anything with those since I realized what they were about."

"How about a time machine? I've heard that you have a time machine."

She threw her head back as far as it would go and laughed. "If I had a time machine, do you think I'd look like this?" Everyone in the studio laughed. "I'd go back before my accident and be a babe. Well, actually, I never was a babe … but, you know."

She was funny! People laughed.

But they didn't laugh when Jon got her to talk about her children. "I've heard it said that your estate is haunted, that you're a witch, and that you have an insane asylum on the property."

Her mouth tightened. "Only the latter is true." She looked over the audience. "I'm sure that people in this audience have loved ones who are mentally ill. People in this audience, and people in the television audience, and out in the world know what it's like to love dear ones who will never be 'normal' according to everyone else's standards.

"You know too how hard it is to get them good treatment. How insurance companies don't cover mental illnesses, or if they do, they cover them at inadequate levels. You'll know how expensive the drugs are, creating profits of thousands of percent for the drug manufacturers.

Those of you with ill children know how people run from your darlings, or make fun of them.

"It's 1997, not the Middle Ages. You'd think things would have changed, but they haven't. All five of my children have incurable mental illnesses. I have the means to give them the best care on the planet. And I do. In a totally legal, modern hospital that I created at my home. I'm fortunate that I have the means to do so. I can treat my family and other unfortunates. I take in other patients and give them the best care.

"I guard my privacy and that of my family carefully. I'm not an open and easy person. I have those dearest in the world to me to look out for. I know all of you will understand that. You've had your own difficulties, your own problems that have no solution. We mothers do the best we can."

Tears ran down her cheeks, but she held her head high. She looked noble, someone everyone could identify with. The aunt or grandmother everyone wished they'd had. Jon let the camera linger on her tearful, but unbroken face, just an instant. The screen faded to a commercial break.

"Vanessa, *dear*, you were magnificent." Mrs. Naughton sat next to her on the sofa, a rumpled tissue in her hand, "And Vanessa, I'll call you *dear* if I want to. We've known each other forever."

"Oh, Marjory," Vanessa held out her arms. "Yes, we are far beyond formality, aren't we? How can I be such a prig? Please call me *dear* whenever you want."

The doorbell rang. Butler brought in a manila envelope. "A delivery from Mr. Walker, ma'am."

Vanessa read Jon's note, which was clipped to the draft of an article:

I contacted *NET WORTH* about the article they had scheduled about you for their Richest Person issue. Since their usual writer, Percival Palimpsest has not met his deadline and they can't find him, I told them I had an alternate piece for the issue and had run a segment on my show about you today. They watched the video and loved it, so *NET WORTH* has agreed to run my attached article, subject to your approval. A contract signed by me is enclosed, if you like what I've written. The photos are yours.

Vanessa took the new text into her study. The art department of Jon's TV station had done a mock-up of the cover and included a few informal shots for the article. She looked beautiful. Her eyes widened as she read. One hand went to her chest.

"Oh, my goodness." She kept reading, breathing harder. "I had no idea he felt this way about me. Marjory! Oh, Marjory! Come and read what Jon said."

"The Richest Person in the World 1997"
Jon Walker © 1997 All rights reserved

"I wish that Vanessa Schierman was my mom. My real mom's a wonderful person, but knowing Dr. Schierman has shown me the lengths to which a mother's devotion and love can go." Jon talked about her children and what she'd done for them a bit, in terms so kind and understanding that anyone reading the piece would tear up.

"I've known Dr. Schierman since I began as Will Duane's private chef. Cooking for her many times at his estate, she corrects my etiquette and presentation of food to this day. The woman knows her forks and knives.

"She's been a shadowy figure in San Francisco's elite, belonging to all the right clubs, yet seen only when she wants to be. Everyone who knows her respects her, though many have only the faintest notion why.

"They may think it's because of her name: Her family was among the original robber barons who seized the budding California economy by might as much as by right. The name still carries a powerful aura.

"Those in financial circles know more about her influence. They may find a deal falling apart or coming together, almost as though a hidden hand had been waved. It's not the hidden hand of the market. It's Vanessa Schierman's hand. Few come to know that.

"Her friendship with Will Duane is probably the best-known facet of Dr. Schierman's life. She's seen with Will at various clubs and events. Most people think *she's* under his umbrella. The friendship in fact, goes the other way. Back in the fifties, he was a Stanford student and she was his mentor.

"If she's been richer than he all this time, why not let the world know? I asked her that and she answered, showing the unobtrusive poise of the truly upper class.

"'Jon, once upon a time not so long ago, flashing one's net worth was in bad taste. You know, vulgar. I was raised to be modest and not to display every dime I had. And I don't. But one day last year, I saw Will's photo on a magazine cover.

"'That photo got to me. Why should he and all the others get the recognition, when the title has been mine for so many years? Did I have to be *so* private? What was I hiding?

"'And so, I approached *NET WORTH* and now I'm talking to you.'

"What do you intend to do now that you've come out?"

"'Nothing. Business as usual. Life as usual.'"

"In your case, that's lots of business."

"'Ah, Jon. In my case, my business is none of your business.'"

The article would be published. Her intuition told her how important it would be for Jon. His star would begin a meteoric rise. What he said left her problems handled, except for the lamentable Mr. Percival Palimpsest in her basement.

"He tore up the curtains, Dr. Schierman, and stuffed them in the commode; that's where the smell comes from. He kept using it, stuffed like that. He's torn up the mattress and tried to light fires. Won't drink anymore milk drinks." George Yeoman filled her in as they traveled down the staircases. "He's claimin' all sorts o' things an' threatenin' hell and worse."

"Hmm," she said. The big house had six levels of basements beneath it, unusual anywhere, but in California almost suicidal, as were the brick and stone used to build the enormous mansion. Smart people didn't use those building materials in earthquake country, but the possibility of her home landing on her head bothered Vanessa not at all.

23

"How silly. He was on the upper floor, with a window, even."

"He claims kidnapping and worse."

"I claim that article he wrote was offensive. Let's see what he has to say now. Stay here, George. I've a bit of private business to manage."

"Let me out of here! You have no right! I'm calling my attorney! This isn't a basement! It's a *dungeon!*" Percival was almost insane after being locked in the cellar room. He didn't know how long he'd been there; they kept giving him these drinks that he finally figured out were knocking him out.

"I'm calling my attorney!" He rushed at the gaunt old lady in the doorway, but stopped short, bouncing off something. A glass wall. The old witch stood on the other side, smiling. She'd put an invisible wall up!

"How are you going to call your attorney, Mr. Palimpsest? You can't get out of this room."

"I'll get out if I have to dig myself out." He felt his mouth contort and his lips pull back to expose his teeth, as they tended to do when he was very upset.

"Well, your attempt to escape through the water closet hasn't been too successful." She indicated the revolting toilet.

"Hah! You thought you could do anything and I'd just *take it.*"

"But Mr. Palimpsest, we do not have to bear the stench of the clogged toilet; you do."

"See, I told you. I won't take it! I'll sue you for everything you've got, you old witch. This is unlawful detention. Kidnapping!" Noises came out of his mouth. As time passed, they were less intelligible.

She couldn't deny it. She was holding him against his will. But what to do with him? She couldn't turn him loose. He *would* sue her. And he'd seen the inside of her house and knew something of her powers. He kept raving and scratching at the invisible wall that she'd put up, shrieking that he wouldn't take it. Finally, he pulled off his shoes and socks, his pants and suspenders. She let him run with it, until he got down to his shirt and the bow tie. As he tore at his shirt buttons, the witch in her came out. A naked Percival Palimpsest was more than she could stomach.

"*Enough*, creature! Be still!" The black silk-like ruff around her neck deployed, its poisonous darts protruding, their jeweled and deadly menace apparent. But not to Percival. You had to touch one of them to find out about their venom, by which time you'd be dead. He was on the other side of the wall she'd created to protect both of them and couldn't know about that particular peril. Her wand leapt into her hand, shooting sparks like bullets. Sparks pierced the glass-like veil.

Percival dropped like a stone when one hit him.

"Oh, no." The last thing she wanted was an insane, possibly fatally wounded mediocre journalist in her cellar.

"George," she whispered into the hallway. "There's been an accident."

Her foreman came in, sucking in a breath. "It's not how we do things, Dr. Schierman, but I would suggest a quiet burial. In the lowest level of the basement."

"Oh, George, do you think he's really dead?"

George felt for a pulse. "Yes, ma'am. I think so."

"Are you sure? Maybe he's just stunned?"

"Ma'am, I think I'd get a nice little grave dug for him, just in case."

"Vanity destroys everything, Scottie." She sat on the garden bench with her cats clustered around, begging to be petted. "If I hadn't been jealous of Will, I wouldn't have revealed myself to *NET WORTH*, they wouldn't have sent that creature here, and none of this would have happened."

Scottie jumped onto the bench, purring loud enough to drown out the other cats. "You're the smartest one, aren't you? If you'd been that

Palimpsest person, you would have realized how sensitive I was, and how protective of my children. You would have written an article like Jon's from the start, wouldn't you?"

The cat climbed into her lap and began kneading the front of her bodice with sheathed claws. His yellow eyes peered at hers, full of intelligence, kindness, and understanding.

"You would make a great journalist, Scottie. You comprehend every word I say, don't you?"

Scottie kept purring and kneading, but he bobbed his head, too.

"Oh, my God! That's it!" She sat up straight, but Scottie didn't fall off her lap. "Are you sure, darling? You'd like New York City and traveling all over?" The cat rubbed one cheek and then the other on her bodice, purring louder than any cat ever had. "Really? That's what you want to do?"

She could do it. She knew she could. She'd been experimenting with it for ages.

"Marjory, have the staff ready the White Room." She ran to the door to the basements and called down, "George. Don't bury him yet. Hold up a minute."

"Vanessa, you *can't* use the White Room. It's too soon. It's only been a few weeks since you were in it."

"Marjory, the White Room and everything associated with it are my business. You will not concern yourself."

George Yeoman climbed through the basement door, smelling musty with dirt on his boots. "We were just about ready, Dr. Schierman. Grave all dug."

"Hold on a minute. I may have a better solution."

"Oh, Scottie, you look stunning," Vanessa exclaimed. He inhabited Percival Palimpsest's body beautifully. Its original occupant tended to hunch and stick out both his front teeth and Adam's apple while rubbing his hands together, like a particularly unpleasant rodent.

Scottie was smoothly elegant, glancing around the chamber as if he'd always been human. He rose slowly with quiet authority, even though he'd never stood erect or on two feet before. "We'll put you in the White Room a few days, and you'll acclimate beautifully. All this will make sense," Vanessa said.

"It makes sense already, Vanessa," Scottie said in a silky tone, as though he'd been able to talk all his life. "I've always wanted to be a person. I thought I'd do a better job of it than most." He took an unsteady step toward her.

Scottie put out a hand and touched the chamber's wall. "Dizzy. I do need some time in the White Room." His brilliant, intelligent eyes settled on her. "Do you know what I'm going to miss most, Vanessa? Sitting in your lap and having you pet me."

"It's beautiful," Scottie said as they walked down the pier where the yacht was moored. He'd had a terrible time adjusting to his new name, Percival Palimpsest.

"Anyone would hate that name, dear. That's why you're in the middle of legally changing your name. Remember? We signed the papers. Are you sure you're ready for this?"

"Oh, yes. *NET WORTH* was very clear: I'd blown the interview with you; I'd better replace it with something better. Now. If I want to keep my job."

"Aren't we lucky that Abdul and the boys got you interviews with the sheik and his friends? No one has ever interviewed them. You can yacht out to the islands and meet them.

"But, darling, do come back. You're welcome at my home any time. You can even interview me if you must. You know how much I love you." She embraced his sleek, spare frame with her bony one.

"It was for the best, Vanessa; I was wasted as a cat. I'll make a great journalist. I always tell the truth, but kindly and in good taste. I'll miss you." Scottie allowed himself the tiniest purr. He rubbed his cheek on her collarbone. "I'll make you proud."

"Well, Abdul, you have a mission," she approached her captain, staying as far from the boat as possible on the wharf. "You have to deliver Percival, who likes to be known as Scottie, to the islands and the interview with the sheik. And take this creature," she held out a stinking, dripping cat carrier with a hissing animal inside, "and do whatever you want with him. If he's a good cat, turn him loose on the islands. If he's as rotten as he appears to be now, toss him overboard once you're out to sea. Give us a moment, if you would."

She put the cage on the dock and bent to address the hissing cat inside. "You weren't quite dead, were you, *P-u-r*-c-i-v-a-l? Just stunned. Now you know you shouldn't mess with what you don't understand—or be rude and intrusive. I've said that I don't have a cyclotron or a time machine on my property. That wasn't entirely a lie. No one asked about other bits of technology I might have cobbled together. Or about what *I* could do without technical assistance." She chuckled.

"You could have been an almost dead body buried in my cellar, but you got a chance at a new life through modern physics, and witchery. You could have stayed on my estate as a cat the rest of your life, protected from everything. Cherished maybe, if you had gotten your biting under control.

"But you are as rotten a cat as you were a person. *P-u-u-r*-c-i-v-a-l, they *will* throw you overboard if you don't shape up.

"So *shape up!*" The sheer black ruff around her neck protruded for an instant, with its poison and jewels. She hid her wand in her dress.

The cat made a loud thump as it leapt to the rear of the box.

"That's better. Be a good boy now, *P-u-u-r*-c-i-v-a-l, and you won't end up as shark bait."

"Goodbye, dear." She kissed Scottie's cheek as they prepared to leave the slip. "So long, Abdul! Gentlemen. We'll think of other adventures when you come back."

"We can give you wonderful rides around the bay, ma'am. Not so many waves." Abdul nodded vigorously.

"Oh, no. I wouldn't dream of going ten feet from the slip. But I love my yacht. You have permanent jobs, gentlemen. We'll have other tales to tell."

The *NET WORTH* cover produced by Jon Walker and
approved by Dr. Vanessa Schierman.

A Vanessa Schierman PhD Witch Tale

THE
TALISMAN &
THE WITCH'S CODE
SANDY NATHAN

Two

The Talisman & the Witch's Code

1
THE TALISMAN

1997

Vanessa sat at her dressing table, peering into the looking glass. She *couldn't* look that ugly. But she did. She swiped her fingers over the creases at the corners of her mouth, glancing at the pots of powder and cream on her vanity. She didn't know how to use them to improve her looks. Cosmetics wouldn't be enough, even if she did know how to use them.

She would never get what she longed for. Or whom. He stood next to her in the framed photo on the dressing table. Magnificent, startlingly handsome. Their image had appeared on the cover of *NET WORTH Magazine* the month before.

When she so magnanimously revealed to their blundering reporter that *she* was the richest person in the world, not Will Duane, as *NET WORTH* had erroneously reported for twenty years, the magazine did a joint issue on the two of them: the richest man and woman on the planet.

She sighed as she remembered the glory of the photo shoot. They did it at Will's house, of course. Vanessa didn't tolerate visitors at her estate. A chuckle escaped her, sounding more like a cackle than she would have liked. Visitors didn't tolerate the estate well, either, though most of them came out of their hysterics soon after leaving.

Will's estate was down the hill, in the flatlands of Woodside. Wide open, oak-studded meadows framed the magnificent modern masterpiece–his home. Sunlight flooded the gardens around the pool. The photographers, a passel of them, shot away while Will smiled at her. Charming. Irresistible. So amazingly sexy. Young people thought that those over sixty were all but dead. Not so. Not Will, and certainly not her.

Will smiled and put his arm around her, gazing into her eyes with his clarity and intelligence flaming. He had treated her like a princess, as though she were his best friend.

That was definitely not what she wanted.

"You mean so much to me, Vanessa. If you hadn't taken me under your wing years ago, I'd still be a garbage collector's son—or *waste management contractor's* son—wondering why I couldn't get anywhere in the San Francisco Bay Area." He smiled, making light of his humble beginnings. "You showed me what really mattered in upper class society—grammar and spelling."

"And excellent table manners, as well as proper pronunciation," she added gleefully. "As well as *entre* into the best clubs, and references—no, glowing endorsements—from those already in power. Preferably at the high end of power." She sniffed and raised her head. Vanessa couldn't help being a snob.

The splendid day was almost ruined by a foolish photographer. The magazine was on a tight time schedule for publication, so the workers toiled in Will's basement office, generating proofs for them to approve then and there. She and Will had previously had legal contracts drawn requiring their signed acceptance of images for publication. Vanessa hadn't had any photos published before this shoot, but she knew she'd need legal protection if it ever happened.

"*I had to photoshop the* shit *out of that picture to make her look human,*" a wretched little dimple on a laptop whispered to her co-worker. The dimwit had no idea how acute a witch's hearing was. *"I'd swear she was a witch, but I didn't think they came that ugly. Look, I put the final version on this tablet."*

Vanessa stiffened and shot a hard look at the vicious photographer. The girl's hands flew to her throat. She began choking as Vanessa grabbed the tablet from her hands.

"How do you make this work?" She shook the unit and the picture covered the wall. "Oh. That is quite large."

Vanessa had not been completely aware of what photoshop was, or what it could do. Photoshopping had worked miracles. The photographer had apparently removed her head, tilted the chin down and moved the whole thing back on her neck. She'd taken away the hump on Vanessa's back. The protrusion had grown year by year since the accident. Her horse had fallen on the hunt field decades earlier. It ended the poor dear's life and broke Vanessa's back. They couldn't fix it in those days; she survived, but her head leaned forward, looking like it might topple from her neck.

But that nasty sprite with the camera and laptop had fixed all that, on paper anyway. The little snit, who was gasping and holding her throat while Vanessa reviewed her handiwork, had smoothed the ravines and craters of Vanessa's face and tamed the protuberance of her chin. She looked handsome, if not lovely. It was enough.

"Very nice. I approve it." Vanessa handed the tablet to the girl, releasing her spell. The child couldn't speak, but Vanessa did. "Haven't you heard the saying, 'If you can't say something nice, don't say anything at all'? It's most useful. You should try it for a while. In fact, you will."

Vanessa didn't look at Will's image at all. No need—he would appear as he always did: magnificent. Glowing. Brilliant. Tantalizing. White hair and dark blue eyes shimmering with intellect. She glanced at the photo of the two of them on her vanity. Will was tall, even next to her photoshopped self.

Why didn't he love her?

He never noticed her next to the perfect, if vacuous, bimbos he "dated." She sniffed, knowing full well what *bimbo* meant and the behavior that accompanied the appellation. Would he love her if she looked and acted like that?

If she were beautiful, she'd still be as smart as she was. Vanessa was a theoretical physicist, one of the best back in the 1930s. She and Will had educated conversations about everything: stock markets, the supply of money, the Federal reserve rate. They could even talk about art and history. Will was an art collector and she had supervised her family's collections of treasures for ages. They spoke about modern political history with vigor. Vanessa had lived far longer than she'd admit. She'd participated in large chunks of modern history, knowing it firsthand. She and Will had a crackling intellectual relationship. They enjoyed each other's company.

Why couldn't he love her?

Because she was a hideous, terrifying old witch who scared the crap out of most people, to use the popular parlance.

Of course, she hadn't always been this way.

When she'd married Heinrich, she had been a handsome woman. That was many years ago, long before the children and the pain their tragic condition had brought her—and the pain her husband's state had brought as well. Heinrich had turned out to be mentally ill. The dazzle and charm that won her heart was mania. His bipolar disorder could be wonderful on the up side, but when his mood turned downward to depression, it was terrible for her to witness and worse for him to live. She certainly hadn't exercised due diligence in researching her husband.

Why hadn't she realized that she and a German warlock whose name was virtually the same as hers might have genetic incompatibilities? True, his family came from a different part of Germany than hers: Heinrich von Schierman's ancient brood hailed from the prosperous north west of the German nation. Her direct ancestors had fled the old country centuries before. Those who stayed in Germany were from the southeast around the mountains near Switzerland.

But her name was Schierman and her father's name had been Heinrich Schierman and half of his male relatives bore the same surname. Why didn't she realize that her forbearers dropped the "von" in their name to Americanize themselves and erase any ties to their aristocratic roots? Because of passion, of course. The same reason empires rise and fall.

Vanessa Schierman had fallen madly in love with and married Heinrich von Schierman, her distant cousin. Not distant enough. Their children emerged so flawed, so ill. They had aged her as surely as the passage of time. And then the accident left her bent, as she was.

Vanessa sat thoughtfully. Could she morph back in time to look the way she had? Absolutely. Her PhD was not an idle ornament hung behind her name. She'd kept up her experiments long after retiring. In her home laboratory, she'd created things that the planet's military powers would kill to have. She had invented a way to go back to the self she'd been before her marriage. She could go back to whatever time she wanted. Would the rejuvenated Vanessa be lovely enough to tempt Will?

No. Even if she availed herself of the time-bending means at her disposal, she still wouldn't be a babe. Worse, she would end up in the present, in 1998, her brain back in the time she took herself to, with no memory of Will Duane whatsoever. She wouldn't know what had happened between, say, 1950 and now. The memories wouldn't exist in her brain.

Even the platonic friendship that existed between them would be gone. Will wouldn't know who she was. And she'd think him an old man.

She had to find another way.

Heaving herself as erect as she was able, Vanessa steeled herself for another day. How could she make Will see her as a woman? As a mate? As the love of his life?

The hallway outside her private rooms was paneled in dark wood covered with ornate carvings. Swags of flowers and leaves converged into opulent trusses of ribbons and bows—all wooden, yet all moving as though kissed by a breeze. Bewitched, the carvings swayed and little *things* peeped forth. Small whittled animals, squirrels, chipmunks, and a fox or two. A mahogany monkey that she had breathed to life and set loose in the paneling when she was a child. And bats. Vanessa loved bats. They awakened as she headed into the kitchen to greet its familiar human denizens, Mrs. Marjory Naughton, her chief housekeeper and confidant, and Cook, her cook. It was time for breakfast and coffee.

Brilliant sparkles of light cascaded onto the landing and down the stairway. Her mother's portrait was awake. Vanessa turned and saw her mother rendered larger than life and magicked into seeming alive. Her face was cold and regal and icily beautiful, brows arched, lips parted as though about to bestow a curse. Her ruff wafted from her neck, opalescent and pastel-colored with sparkles flying everywhere.

Vanessa's teeth ground together. Her mother had the gaudiest ruff of any witch she knew. It was beyond bad taste. But what did you expect from Euro-trash floating around the continent on a charm and a spell? Her father should have known better; he was the one with the bloodlines and money.

Still, even dead and in a painting, her mother commanded attention. Nothing could outshine her jeweled, beaded, and spangled dress. It cast light like air-kisses, flashes cascading down the landing and entry hall. The wand in her right hand was so flamboyant that it made her clothes and ruff look chaste. Illuminated letters burst from it and fell to the floor, spelling her name: Ophelia. Ophelia. *Ophelia* drifted down to the painted carpet beneath her painted feet.

Vanessa studied the portrait. By coming alive like this, her mother was surely trying to tell her something. What?

Ophelia Schierman's left hand rested on her chest. Above that, the talisman glowed.

The talisman! That was it! It worked subtly, so that its target didn't know it was operating.

Vanessa could cast a spell and Will would idolize her even if she looked like a donkey. She could *make* him do anything. Why not? If you can't compel people to things against their will, what was the use being a witch? She could magick Will into submission and devotion, but that wasn't what she wanted.

She wanted him to love her the way she loved him: knowing his weaknesses and faults, his strengths and essential goodness and kindness—most of which he hid behind a public display of rotten behavior and foul temper. She knew who he really was, and loved all of him.

Beside the grossest enchantment, what could make him love her the same way?

She could use the talisman to subtly charm Will. Not bewitch him, but move the parts of his soul that cared for her to the fore. Let Will's own heart and soul come to her.

"I've got it!" Vanessa cried, bursting into the kitchen.

"Wonderful, dear. Got what?" Mrs. Naughton said. Cook merely handed her a mug of coffee.

"I'll get the talisman. Then everything will work out!"

"The talisman? What talisman?"

"The Blood Talisman. It's mine. My mother took it."

"Where is it?"

"With my mother's corpse—at the family estate in Germany. I'm going there right now."

"Oh! I'd better pack for you, Vanessa. How long will you be gone?"

"Pish! I don't need to pack. I'll be gone as long as it takes!"

Vanessa's tailored ruff emerged from her neck with a subtle sheen of black *peau de soi*, its jet crystal beaded points glittering, but not emitting venom. Her wand appeared in her hand, slightly bigger than perfectly tasteful, but just the way she liked it. Vanessa raised her wand and disappeared.

"What is the Blood Talisman?" Mrs. Naughton asked Cook. They looked at each other and then at the empty space where Vanessa had stood.

2

HOME

The castle's immense entry hall was darker and more somber than she remembered. Of course, it had been eons since she'd visited. Even so, the stillness was weird. The château perched on the edge of a mountain, the kind of dwelling that exists only in the Alps. Huge and impractical, the only reason that it hadn't been converted into a tourist attraction or hotel was that it was so terrifying that even tourists seeking supernatural thrills wouldn't chance it. In the valley below, the fortress's shadow dampened the spirits of all it touched. That and her family was loaded and didn't need to prostitute itself by entertaining paying guests.

But the stronghold had been a turbulent hotbed of life—witches and warlocks weren't the *undead*, after all. They lived and needed servants. She was an only child, but her father's people reproduced like viruses, mutating just as fast. She had phalanxes of cousins and once-twice-thrice removed necromancers calling her *auntie*. She was no one's auntie, but answered to the term when in the ancestral stronghold.

Where was everyone? Vanessa stood alone in the vast stone-walled space. Even her breathing echoed. She looked around, up and down, turned in a circle. Total disaster! No witch worth the name would allow her home to deteriorate so. Ropes and tangles of cobwebs hung everywhere, their eight-legged creators nowhere in sight.

"I'll fix that." She raised her wand and the cobwebs formed braids, festoons, and dainty Germanic lace patterns. A swag of spider silk draped the main entrance. "That's much better. Spiders! Emerge!" A few decrepit specimens appeared, legs broken, sheen gone.

"What has happened to you?"

The same that happened to everything. Look around, came the spiders' silent response.

Vanessa looked around. Tapestries hung over every stone of the wall not covered by ancestor portraits. They depicted the family's favorite subjects: the active subjugation of the working serfs and the conquest of surrounding fiefdoms. The weavings depicted rape and pillage and pogrom-type pursuits that made *The Rape of the Sabine Women* look G-rated.

Normally, the figures on the tapestries acted out what they were depicted as doing, predating large screen and X-rated TV by centuries. Now, the weavings were still, their color dimmed by… something, as well as the spider's webs and dust coating their surfaces.

The same could be said of the ancestor portraits. The figures hung limply in their frames, dejected, lifeless, and not the all-conquering, never-daunted Schiermans she knew. Another thing: most of the furniture and all of the silver and porcelain was missing. The hall was truly empty. What had happened?

Fear shot through Vanessa. Had her relatives pawned the Blood Talisman? She needed that; the crawling tapestries and combatant portraits spelled home, but not her heart's desire.

"Where is everyone?" Her ruff shot out. Her wand filled her hand. *They* knew she needed to be prepared. "Cousins! Nurse! Nanny! Where are you?" She turned slowly, noting the despoliation of a castle that had endured for centuries. "What's happened here?"

"Where are my cousins? It's Vanessa, come from America. Where are you?"

After some time, she heard a rattling tap. Someone was coming from the castle's inner sanctum. Peering down a darkened hallway, she saw an ancient figure tapping her way toward her. *Using her wand as a cane!*

"Cousin Viola! Why are you using your wand like that? Stop, dear! It's a travesty." Vanessa was sufficiently shocked that she forgot that she hated her cousin Viola. She looked so horrible, who wouldn't feel pity? "What's happened?"

"Ah can't say ah know. Who're you?"

"I'm Vanessa Schierman, from California. You know me. We've visited."

The crone looked her up and down. "Ah daresay you've done better than me. Been hard times here."

"How?"

"Don't know, dear. Expect a spell's been cast on me. Think ah'm the last living soul here. Think so."

"Viola! You must remember! What has happened to the castle and all the furniture? And the cousins?"

"All th' fam'ly's gone. 'spect they sold the swag to keep up the lifestyle. Designer this, couture that. Hard to be a witch in modern times."

"It went for *clothes?*" Vanessa stepped back, truly shocked. Her skirt swayed forward, reminding her of her own clothing. This dress was one of her favorites, floor length and completely black with fine pleats and tucks, black lace trim, and obsidian buttons like eyes. Custom made, of course, but by the villagers who lived behind the estate house. Cost nothing.

"Oh, yeah. Y' need t' have top drawer clothes and shoes. Handbags, of course. And posh entertaining. Couldn't do it here." The other witch raised her wrinkled face to indicate the doomsday hanging over them.

"You could if you *cleaned* up a bit. I entertain. I even had a wedding at my house."

"A wedding? Do people still get married?" A demented giggle. "Of course they do. Ah forgot that our Adrianna and Laurenz von Zadicus were married. But not here."

"Where?"

"In Paris. At a fancy hotel. Took the last silver candelabra to pay for it. They're here. Somewhere. They'll come out in a while." She looked up at the narrow gothic windows. A shadow of dim light indicated their location. It was almost dark. "Sleep all day, awake all night. Howling and carrying on."

"Adrianna is here?" That was a blessing. Adrianna was a level head and a smart one. A new breed of witch. Incorruptible. "Who else is here?"

"No one; everyone with any life lit out."

Vanessa cursed silently. "Well, I think I'll go wake her up."

Viola's eyes widened, fit to burst. "Oh, no. Wouldn't do that. She's with Laurenz, y'know. Newlywed." Viola's bulging eyes took on a lascivious glint.

Vanessa certainly didn't want to walk in on her distant cousin in the raptures of the newly conjoined.

"Come in the kitchen with me, Cousin Vanessa. Ah'll make ye a cuppa."

Since when did her relatives start talking like Yorkshiremen? Vanessa followed her. They walked a long way, into a kitchen that might have been cleaned in this century. Or not.

"What happened to the servants? You had a whole village of them, just as I do."

"Too lively for here. Lit out when Laurenz's family started coming by. Now it's just me."

Vanessa washed their cups, and the teakettle, pot, and teaspoons. She wiped down the old stove and the table top and resisted the urge to mop the floor. Viola was obviously very ill; she couldn't keep up. But why not hire someone from town?

Curious as she was about the cause of the degenerated state of the ancestral castle and finances, Vanessa had a mission: get the Blood Talisman and go back home. She sipped tea, glancing at Viola surreptitiously. Her third cousin twice-removed was just as unwilling to make eye contact with *her*. Vanessa knew what she looked like and couldn't blame her, but if the pot ever called the kettle... Viola was no one to feel superior regarding looks.

"I've come to see everyone, of course, but I do miss Mama so. I wanted to visit her crypt and bring her these..." Bring her what? A bouquet of deadly nightshade leapt into Vanessa's hand. Being a witch was so useful. "A token of respect. Mama is still in the mausoleum, I suppose? You haven't found it necessary to pawn her remains to buy new shoes or anything?"

The other witch made a disgusting snort. "Pawn *your* mother? Like to see the bloke who'd try that madness. She's got a circle of demons around her. Good thing, too, because Laurenz an' them want that jewel on her throat. Covet it bad. But Ophelia's as much a witch dead as she was alive."

Relief bathed Vanessa. She'd nip down to the crypt, grab the jewel, and be off. Pity to miss seeing Adrianna, but she'd undoubtedly enjoy her tryst with her new husband more than a cup of tea with her "auntie."

"Well, I don't suppose I'll have any problem. The jewel is rightfully mine, as the female head of our line. I'll just..." She rose to leave when she spied an emaciated waif wearing an almost invisible chemise in the doorway.

"Adrianna? Is that you?" The creature was almost naked. "Viola, grab a table cloth or something to cover her. She's lost her clothes..."

"What?" the waif objected. "This is a *Vermilini Couture* gown."

"Gown? It's barely a handkerchief..." Vanessa took the cloth Viola proffered and wrapped it around the urchin's shoulders. "What happened to you? You were such a robust girl." Now skin and bone, pale as death, Adrianna had once sported thick glossy hair that curled and bounced. But now nothing about her indicated any life within her. She kept her eyes down and averted.

"Thin is in, auntie. You should know that. Laurenz and I travel a great deal all over the world. We move in fashionable circles. I have to look the part."

"Well, society has changed a great deal since I was a girl. A woman had to have recognizable boobs back then." The other witches recoiled at her words. "Boobs and an ass. You look like a drowned rat."

Adrianna shot a look at her. Something about it alarmed Vanessa, but the young witch turned away before she could puzzle it out.

"One thing hasn't changed," the scrawny duck's wispy voice had an edge, a definite bite. "People of breeding have *manners*. They don't 'drop in' uninvited and make judgments about family and home. We haven't seen you since your mother died, and you come here, saying all these things..."

How did Adrianna hear her and Viola talking closeted away in the ancient kitchen? Was the house bugged? That was likely. Vanessa's mansion certainly was. Was her witch's hearing especially acute? Or was she something else? A horrible thought was coming to Vanessa. The only thing with better hearing than a witch was a...

"Oh my God!" She spun to the door. Another wasted figure stood there, this one male with lank, dark hair. He wore trousers like those popular in the 1800s and nothing else. His skin gleamed white and his eyes flashed red.

"AAAAAAAA!" The war cry emerged from her with no stops, no holding back. Her hair stood on end, mouth flashing her teeth. Vanessa's ruff jumped two feet from her neck, poison acid squirting from its jeweled tips at the interloper. The poison alone should have killed him, but her wand settled the matter conclusively.

Shooting from her hand, its handle formed a T, or more correctly, a cross. The business end of the wand hit the stranger just to the left of the breast bone, piercing his body at the heart. Before she could even say, *"How do you do, Laurenz? Welcome to the family,"* the rotter lay dead on the kitchen floor. Nothing like a stout oak wand for offing vampires.

Viola and Adrianna stared at her, lips retracting from their fangs and bloodshot eyes glinting ruby in the dim light. The wand ejected itself from Laurenz's chest and flung itself at Viola's, finding the same deadly perch. The older witch fell, black blood leaking from her wound. Vanessa's wand pulled itself from Viola's body and hovered over Adrianna.

Adrianna dropped to her knees, hissing. She crawled toward Vanessa, hissing and threatening with her teeth. Before she got very far, her body began to sway back and forth between her aunt and her husband. Growing still, she wailed, "You *killed* Laurenz. You killed my *husband.*"

Her grief didn't last long; leaping to her feet, Adrianna dropped the table cloth shielding her fragile body and pointed at Vanessa. The older witch jerked back, feeling the curse and spell cast upon her. Becoming a vampire hadn't hurt her young relation's witching ability one bit.

"You killed my husband. You *owe* me." The waif's face was set and ugly. "You owe me until the end of time."

Sadly, that was true. It was the way of witches.

3
THE WAY OF VAMPIRES

"How *could* you get involved with a vampire, Adrianna? They're disgusting. All that lurking about, rolling their eyes and leering. And so messy! Blood everywhere. Witches and vampires have been enemies forever. How could you *marry* one?"

After incinerating Laurenz and Viola, the finally-really-dead undead, and adding twenty pounds of flesh and a bathrobe to Adrianna's emaciated frame–all with a bit of fancy wand work–Vanessa sat at the kitchen table drinking tea with her distant cousin.

Adrianna choked on her Earl Grey tea. "Vampires don't eat or drink… human food, Auntie."

"You sure as hell will, Missy. Or *Mrs*. I won't have anyone thinking you're one of *those*. No, you're anorexic and anemic, but not undead. Drink! And tell me what ransom you want to extract from me."

"You know the witch's code: if a witch kills another witch's husband, the killer is bound to do all that she's asked until she finds the widow another spouse."

"Yes, the offending party must act as a servant until the poor victim is shacked up again. Humph." Vanessa rattled around the inside of her tea cup with a spoon. She narrowed her eyes. "Is that how you got involved with that bloodsucker? You were dragged into it by your genitals?"

Tears formed in Adrianna's eyes. She nodded yes, and the tears drifted down her cheeks.

"Don't give me that, girl, you always had the honing instincts of a barracuda. What was he? Rich? Titled? Did he ply you with drugs and alcohol? Promise you a fortune? Why did you give in?"

"He said he was rich and he is titled. It was a big party at his castle… I'd never done drugs before."

"Pish."

"Well, *those* drugs." She got a misty, far-away look. "It was so romantic. I wore my *Merci-Boubou* gown and *Jimmy Hamm* shoes. My *Pricey-tot* bag. I had my hair and makeup done in Monte Carlo. Everyone at the party was so glamorous. I was finally in the crowd I wanted to be with. Laurenz was the sexiest man I'd ever seen…"

"*Really?*"

"Oh, yes, that European ambisexual look is the thing this year."

"Humph. From what I saw, he was the most ambisexual man possible."

"Oh, yes, Auntie. He was known as the best lover in Europe, everyone said so, men and women."

"Oh, good. So he seduced you with drugs in an Euro-trash orgy and then made you undead."

"Well, yes. But it was more romantic than that. But that's what it was, really. It wasn't until…" Her red eyes glinted.

"He drained you dry and he and his friends had you six ways from Sunday that you found out he was a vampire and the castle wasn't his."

"And all his friends were vampires."

"And penniless. So you came here and destroyed a dynasty stretching back centuries, in what, a couple of years?"

"Less than that. Months." Her pupils gleamed like a white rabbit's, but they were anything but gentle. This child was far from over her flirtation with blood sucking.

"What do you want from me?"

"What you owe me. A new husband."

"What shall I do, advertise in the *London Times*, 'pretty anorexic vampire seeks mate'? You'll be hard to match, Adrianna."

"Not for you. You're the richest person in the world. I saw that magazine. I want you to take me back to Silicon Valley and hook me up with a venture capitalist or someone with enough money to satisfy my needs."

"And lots of blood, I would assume."

"I'll take care of that. Someone with taste and class who has sophisticated desires that he isn't afraid to express." Adrianna pinched her lip between her fangs. A drop of black blood drifted downward. "And limitless funds."

"Oh, wonderful, just what the Valley needs. You can't come to my home, Adrianna. I won't allow it, and the earth of the estate will spit you out like a bad seed."

"Then put me up in a hotel. The Ritz Carlton will do. It won't take me long, just introduce me to the right man. I'll do the rest."

Vicious, angelic, sexier than was legal: that's what her smile was. Vanessa blanched. A plague bigger than the AIDS epidemic was about to be released on the San Francisco Bay Area. Was there anything she could do? No, the witch's code was the witch's code.

"Let's go," said the vampire princess, her eyes fixed on Vanessa's throat, where her carotid artery throbbed.

Vanessa put her hand to her throat. Lord in heaven! She'd have to fear for her own safety. Adrianna demonstrated that a witch could be a vampire, too. *She* was the nearest living body–and therefore a possibility for lunch.

"I want to go now. Let's project back to Woodside."

"We can't do that."

"Why?"

"I have things to do. Fix up this castle for one thing. I can't leave my ancestral home like this. Even the witch's code wouldn't permit it." And she had to visit the castle library to see what spells could turn a witch who was also a vampire back into just a witch. Perhaps one existed. And what extenuating circumstances that would allow her to break the hold Adrianna had put on her. Vanessa could convene the Continental Coven, perhaps. She was sure that the Sisters would favor her cause. Witches *did* hate vampires. Adrianna's marriage to Laurenz was unnatural in all ways.

And she had to nab her mother's talisman so that the amulet could carefully lure Will Duane into *her* bed without him feeling supernatural forces were at play.

"Wait a minute! The witch's code says you have to do what I say!"

"Screw the witch's code, you little monster." Vanessa's ruff projected and her wand jumped into her hand. "There are witches and there are *witches*. I am a Witch, a senior, mature witch. I can break your spell like that." She snapped her fingers.

"When I have finished my work here, I will escort you to a suitable hotel and set you up with appropriate clothing..."

"And money!" The red bunny eyes shone.

"And money, and then set about finding someone who suits your needs. I am doing this out of the goodness of my heart, not your silly incantation. Although I think Laurenz was hideous and perverted, as well as a vicious murderer condemning his victims to eternal hell, he was your husband. As soon as I finish my work and find a means of removing the vampire from your soul, we'll leave. Now, leave me alone."

"But I'm hungry..."

"Why don't you go out in the woods and slaughter some wild animals? Or be a vegan: chew roots and berries for their juice." Vanessa turned majestically and headed for the library.

4

CLEANING UP

Vanessa knew she had a problem long before she got to the library.
Along the hallways, the remaining furniture lay in broken heaps. How
anything could shatter a solid oak seventeenth century armoire was
beyond her. It was built to house *armor*. The cobwebs moaned and
shrunk from her, or clung to her skirt in terror. The bats looked down
from the massive ceiling beams, eyes glinting. Were they rabid, or
vampires? They weren't her beloved bats.

When she closed the peaked and arched library doors behind her,
Vanessa surveyed the true fall of the house of Schierman. Motes of light
rotated, playing over the scene and illuminating the whole disaster.

The library rose to the peak of the tower, who knew how many
stories. Ladders reached into the stacks of shelves like beseeching arms,
disappearing into the gloom. Torn and ravaged books lay about, thrown,
hacked, destroyed. This was the work of fiends. Illiterate fiends who had
no idea of the treasures held here. Centuries of arcane knowledge. Spells
that would reverse the vampire affliction that Adrianna displayed. The
secrets of the universe, despoiled and torn. This was the true Schierman
treasure that that the bloodsucking Euro-trash had demolished.

The pages began wailing when she entered. "Hush. Hush. I will
mend you. I will set this place right." Vanessa's wand shot out and she
prepared to go to work, when a beam of light fell across her hand...

Where was the light coming from? She cocked her head back and
scanned the walls. The book shelves were interrupted by tall, thin Gothic
windows like the rest of the castle. Their glass panes were outlined by the
stone walls and book cases; the windows were pitch black arches. It was
midnight outside; not even moonlight entered through them.

She gasped as she realized the danger she was in. Why had she assumed that Adrianna and the two vampires she'd killed were the only bloodsuckers in the place? Adrianna had said that her husband's friends traveled in packs. That they had come to the castle when their credit and welcome wore out everywhere else. What if Adrianna and company were just the early risers?

Thumping heard beyond the stout oaken doorway alerted her to the fact that the flimsy blood suckers might have more substantial friends: trolls and ogres, perhaps. Maybe even, perish the thought, zombies.

"Oh, they're so over-done. In *such* bad taste." But they were out there. Something was moaning and pounding on the door. Vanessa raised her wand, which flashed and shot flaming venom in a most reassuring manner. She began:

"Praebet amicis tabulas et cathedras, ostia et cotes timerent magis ausculta quod loquor. Nunc pugnare! Facite vobis in cruce! Cruces; Delebimus enim locum istum qui in vola! Percussisti cor!"

Vanessa preferred Latin for incantations, but she repeated her command in English and German, just in case. "Oaken friends, tables and chairs, doors and shelves, hear me. Now is the time to fight! Make yourselves into crosses! Many crosses! Fly into those who would destroy this place! Strike their hearts and strike them dead! NOW!"

As the last phrases left her lips, the library doors splintered and flew inward.

"UHHUH! UHHUH!" The zombie stumbled toward her, slobbering, arms reaching. Stinking. Incoherent.

"Oh, God. Not those things." What worked against zombies? "Oaken friends, attack him! Them." Others stumbled after the first. "Dear Lord, how do you kill zombies?" The pages of the ruined books began rustling, looking up answers.

"Beat them, lady. Beat their heads in, until they're mush," whispered voices arose from the historic volumes.

"That's too messy. I don't have any spare clothes. And I'm against violence, sort of."

"Or shoot them," came helpful phrases from far up the book stacks.

"I don't have a gun." Her eyes narrowed. "But I do have this." Her wand began firing off electrical impulses like lightning strikes. Zombie heads exploded. "That should be sufficient to disable even the hardiest zombie."

Hordes of bats, vampire bats, poured in the doorway over the stinking, decapitated undead. She could see skeletal forms in designer clothes behind them. The vampires!

"Praebet amicorum! Nunc in hora! Find lamia! Ejice vos in cordibus suis: Vindica te violati patria!

"Oaken friends! Now is the hour! Kill the vampires! Drive yourselves into their hearts! Avenge yourself for the desecration of your home!"

The tables and chairs, bookshelves and armoires, everything oaken, leapt into the air and broke into shards. They transformed into a mighty flying army of crosses. They tore out the door, into the hall and throughout the castle, searching out vampires wherever they might hide.

"Kill the bloodsuckers. All of them. Except Adrianna!" She turned to the matter at hand: the rest of the zombies. They were easy. She blew off their heads. The ogres and trolls followed. They could have been harder, but she had her own ogres and trolls at her estate and knew how to manage them.

"Listen, I know you've had a hard time. Since the vampires came, the neighborhood has gone to hell. Anyone can see that. You need a good manager to set things right. *I* am that manager."

The issue of *NET WORTH Magazine* with her and Will Duane on the cover leapt up from a library table, displaying itself to the assembled monsters. Vanessa felt relieved; things were going her way. The rest were reasonable.

"Who can help you better than me, the richest woman in the world? I know you're upset. Your living standards are in free fall. You probably haven't eaten in ages. Your gold and treasure have been stolen." She drew herself erect and crossed her arms over her chest, wand held in readiness. "I bet that pollution and filth even flows through the mote and under your bridges. I wager that you can't sleep for the reek."

The trolls wailed at that, some breaking down hysterically, to be comforted by their fellows.

Vanessa shook her head sadly. "It's that bad, my dear ones? I suspected it. Well, when the water supply goes, the whole society is not far behind.

"And food. I know that many of you enjoy a good side of beef now and again. The bloodsuckers undoubtedly drained the cattle dry." Wails arose. "You're *starving*. I don't blame you for being irritable when you first saw me.

"I can help you, dear ones. I'm not like a politician who promises the moon and delivers… diddly squat." She stood, eyes closed, weaving on her feet, wand partly raised. The group froze. She spoke when she came back to herself.

"You'll find a herd of healthy cattle by the moat. They're from my ranch in the American West. Do not harvest them all at once! Before I leave, I will teach you sustainable beef production practices, and instruct you in maintaining the quality of your water supply. And I'll teach you how to prevent scourges like the vicious ghouls and vampires from taking over again. Never be fooled by designer clothes and snobbish ways, darlings! They are from the Evil One." The trolls and ogres stared spellbound. They apparently had thought *she* was the Evil One.

"Oh, my dears. I am not the Evil One. His name is Enzo Donatore and he lives in Spain, mostly. You can find out about him elsewhere. I am a Witch! A White Witch, dedicated to goodness and light. I will handle the little problem we find ourselves embroiled in, with *your* help. But *you* are the ones who will make sure it never happens again.

"To those of you who thought I was a namby-pamby pacifist, I am not. I am a pacifist, unless it's stupid to be one. *And I am* never *namby-pamby!*" She roared the last words.

"Now get off your flabby asses and help me clean up this place."

"Oh, Marjory, it's been *awful.*" Vanessa sat at the castle's kitchen table with her housekeeper and dear friend, Marjory Naughton. "I had to project you over from my estate to be with me. I couldn't be alone anymore."

"Don't worry, dear, I find projection so much handier than international flights. No customs and being body searched because of my artificial knee. Anything I can do, I'd be happy to. Although I'm glad you waited until the vampires were mostly gone to call me."

She had told Marjory about Adrianna being a vampire and everything else.

"You *have* to help her?" Marjory asked.

"As far as I can tell. I reconstituted the library and couldn't find a thing about undoing elements of the witch's code or removing the vampire from a living witch. If she had been dead, it would have been no problem."

Marjory smiled perkily. "Well, I don't suppose you could kill her? No..." She played with the necklace of oak crosses Vanessa had given her. "You're sure these will protect me?"

"Yes, as long as I'm here and she's on a different continent."

Marjory looked stricken.

"A joke, my dear."

"Wasn't funny, Vanessa. Let's get to work."

"All right, all of you! Show me what European trolls and ogres can do! Vanessa's California troops can put in a good day's work. They'd clean up this mess in hours. What will *you* do?" Marjory Naughton supervised an army of monsters cleaning up the castle and restoring the water supply.

While Adrianna sulked, Vanessa made a few calls:

"Quae omnia pulchra illicite venduntur argentum et Sinis decoravit Shierman quae olim castrum venit! Venite senex iam et alibi. Lamia abierunt tutum!"

Her calls went through the ethers, not the phone lines: "All the beautiful things that were sold illegally, the silver and china, everything that once graced the Schierman Castle: come home! Come home now and take your old places. The vampires are gone, it is safe! And the gold and jewels that belonged to the trolls and ogres: come home! They miss you."

And then to the scattered relatives and servants, if any: *"Bonum veneficas Schierman in linea! Calones ad arcem et servi! Venite si non lamia. Si lamia, abscondere in terminos universae terrae. Vivamus Schierman de ea!"*

"Good witches of the Schierman line! Servants and retainers at the castle! Come home if you are not a vampire. If you are a vampire, run to the end of the earth and hide. Vanessa Schierman commands it!"

Things shaped up fast after that. Some of the relatives had merely run off rather than becoming undead. After giving the whole place—human, witch, warlock, troll, or ogre—a good talking to about discerning good from evil as well as maintaining a sustainable existence and caring for the castle and their wealth, she, Marjory, and the little trollop were ready to project home.

"Vanessa, have you forgotten something?" Marjory said.

"What, my dear friend?" Vanessa had been staring at Adrianna. The still-undead-but-looking-more-presentable vampire clutched the issue of NET WORTH *Magazine* with her and Will on the cover. She didn't like the look on Adrianna's face as she took in Will Duane's magnificence. Marjory cleared her throat. "What have I forgotten, dear?"

"The Blood Talisman," the housekeeper whispered hoarsely.

"Oh, no! *That!*"

5
THE BLOOD TALISMAN

Vanessa hated the way the way her belly quivered involuntarily whenever she approached her mother. The woman terrified her, even long dead, and in spite of the fact that Vanessa had proven herself the supreme witch in the family when she was three years old. On her third birthday, she had bewitched her parents and forced them to give up their philandering and cruelty.

She couldn't help it: her mother had cut off the head of the pony given to her as a birthday present. She'd melted her birthday cake. Vanessa was so angry that her ruff burst out of her neck and her wand appeared: the unerring signs of a witch emerging, though the great event happening to a three-years-old was precocious. Her spell stopped her parents' evil ways and made them good parents. Or as good as possible; even witchcraft isn't 100%. She restored the pony and the cake.

Things got easier in the family after that, but not cozy. Just before her mother died, instead of graciously handing the priceless amulet to its rightful owner–Vanessa, the new leader of the lineage–her mother had stolen it and nipped off to the castle in Germany. Then she died, demanding to be put up in style for all eternity, wearing the talisman.

Now, her mother lay in state in the castle's crypts. Vanessa loved the crypts, but her feelings boiled like one of her concoctions. Magnificent stone pillars and arches cut into the solid rock under the castle held the remains of hundreds, maybe thousands, of years of dead Schiermans. And her mother.

Ophelia Schierman wasn't royalty. She hadn't even been rich. She wasn't a Schierman. She was the past century's equivalent of the little trollop Adrianna had become. Euro-trash was such a perfect word to describe people who carelessly ranged around the continent, spending more than they had and living wasted and fruitless, if stylish, lives.

Which is what her mother had done until her father ran afoul of her web of spells and fell in love with her forever. Mother had been a beautiful witch, dauntingly sexy and stylish, and undoubtedly had skills in areas that Vanessa didn't want to contemplate. Papa remained smitten all his life. He wasn't faithful, of course, but he did pretty well, especially after Vanessa bewitched him.

Her mother's enchantment had affected her husband past both of their deaths; this was his family's castle, not hers. Yet her father lay at home in California in a simple crypt while she got the star treatment in the ancestral tomb. But who could deny Ophelia Schierman what she wanted, dead or alive?

Vanessa made her way deeper into the gloom until she reached the penultimate spot, the deepest depths, a grotto in the stone. There her mother was, lying on a granite dais covered with a crystal case. She reminded Vanessa of the grizzly bear her father had shot and had mounted, except that it stood erect.

Her mother's flawless face was as beautiful as if she lay napping. Her gaudy ruff lay limp around her head and the jewels of her gown throbbed in a subdued fashion. She still terrified Vanessa, despite her own power and accomplishments. She always felt like the ugly, stupid swan-chick that would never transform when compared to her mother.

Vanessa had to focus on what she was doing: she could see the beautiful talisman pinned to the fabric covering her mother's breast. Her opalescent hands crossed beneath it.

"Mama," she whispered, curtsying before the form under the glass cover and peering at her mother's face. Ophelia looked better than she had alive. Vanessa sighed, losing momentum. *"Grab it and get out of here,"* a voice whispered inside. "Mama, I need the Talisman. It wasn't really yours. You took it from me. I'm the head of the family now. I'm taking it back."

The jewel rose from her mother's chest and passed through the crystal barrier, landing in Vanessa's hands. She stared at it.

"Darling, I was a rotten mother. We know that. I stole the jewel from you, that is true. Now you have it and can use it as it was supposed to be used. Vanessa, you are everything I could wish for in a daughter. You're brave and kind and generous. You are a good friend. I wish you well. I love you."

Vanessa clutched the amulet and ran. She was hallucinating.

"You've got it?" Marjory asked her when Vanessa staggered into the kitchen.

"Yes."

"Was it hard?"

"Yes, worse than fighting zombies." She told her friend what had happened.

Marjory's face screwed up in disbelief. "She said that?"

"Must have been her. I don't think I was really hallucinating. Do you?"

"You're the least likely to hallucinate person I know. We need to go back to California. I've made arrangements for…" Marjory tossed her head in the direction of Adrianna's room. "She's packing. I've got her a suite at the Ritz Carlton in Half Moon Bay. It's close enough to the estate for us to keep an eye on her. I've got George Yeoman organizing the villagers to watch her so that she doesn't… imbibe too many of the hotel guests and locals. We're getting it organized, Vanessa." Marjory's jaw clenched and her eyes narrowed. "But there's a problem."

"What?" But she already knew.

"This," Marjory held up the *NET WORTH Magazine* cover with the photo of Will and Vanessa on it. "She wants *him*. Says marrying Will is the only way she can be repaid for your murdering her husband."

"Lord in heaven!" Vanessa plopped into a chair. "I have to do what she wants. What am I to do, Marjory?"

"You'll introduce him to me and let me do the rest," Adrianna said, walking into the kitchen. Servants staggered behind her, bearing

Adrianna's trunks. "I do know my job. He will be unable to resist me." The little sow smiled, not bothering to dim the red gleam in her eyes or hide her fangs. She looked much better; her skin was close to normal in tone and she was slim, not skeletal. But Adrianna was still was a vampire––and a witch.

"Let's go."

6

STALKING WILL

"This isn't bad." Adrianna pulled open the draperies of her suite and admired the Pacific Ocean outside. The spacious rooms were luxuriously appointed in muted neutrals that perfectly complemented the sea's shifting hues. "I should have visited Auntie long ago."

"You wouldn't have been welcome. You're not welcome now," Marjory Naughton said. She was babysitting their young visitor while George Yeoman, the leader of the villagers, arranged round the clock coverage of the vampire. They couldn't have her murdering people willy-nilly right outside the Schierman estate's walls. Vanessa's five thousand acres draped over Woodside's skyline, coming close to the ocean in places. "If you have any sense, you'll drop this nonsense and leave Vanessa alone. She's better than you in every way and doesn't deserve your harassment. Go back to Germany."

Adrianna bridled. "Watch your tongue! You are not a Schierman. Remember who I am. And what I can do."

"Oh, I'll never forget that." Marjory sniffed and raised her head, fondling the necklace of wooden crosses around her neck. They stood tensely, facing each other. A knock on the door broke the strain. "That will be George. He's brought dinner for you. He will keep you supplied; you are *not* to molest any people or pets."

George tipped his cap. A couple of the village men followed him into the suite bearing wire mesh crates. "We got ye some nice rabbits and squirrels. That's the best we could do with short notice."

"You expect me to live on wild rabbits and squirrels? Those are barely suitable for peasants. I want a…"

"Well, ma'am, we're out to catch a wild boar. We'll get 'im and bring 'im to you on the morrow."

"And deer. Get me a deer. I prefer fawns, if I have to eat *game*."

George looked at her, his stocky peasant's body radiating his displeasure and power. "Y're not one t' be callin' the shots, girl. Not w' me or my people, or Dr. Schierman, either. Y're lucky she don't do what she did to that—"

"That's enough, George. I expect that Adrianna will find out what Vanessa can do soon enough." Marjory turned to Adrianna, pulling several sheets of paper from her satchel. "This is your schedule for the week. Tomorrow, we will go shopping at Stanford Shopping Center. You need proper clothes if you are to meet Mr. Duane."

"I have proper clothes. All my clothes are top designers: *Cash Box, Vetienne Vitieni, Mamo J*. Top name couture."

"You look like you raided the lingerie chest of a high priced… woman of the night. Will Duane will not like you if you look like an… evening's entertainment for hire."

Adrianna blinked. "Really?"

"Tomorrow we shop. Then we get you enrolled in school."

"School?"

"Yes, Mr. Duane is extremely productive and performance-orientated. If you are to 'visit' your 'auntie' for any length of time, you will need to be fruitfully employed. It's school or get a job."

"A *job*?"

"I know it's hard to understand, Adrianna, but in Silicon Valley, people *work. Everyone works. Even babies work*. They have classes and things nonstop from birth. That's why they succeed."

"Really?"

"Yes. George has people guarding your room—to keep you in. I will leave you to your dinner. Please do not mess up the room; eat in the shower and clean up after yourself. The cost of anything you bloody or destroy will come out of your allowance."

"I have an allowance?"

"Yes, based on your performance. It's called 'pay.' I administer it."

"Why am I doing things with you? Why isn't Auntie here?"

Both Marjory and George Yeoman bridled. "You've done enough to her, Adrianna. You will do no more. *We* are your handlers."

When Marjory arrived back at the estate, she found Vanessa in the living room, distraught. She paced and wrung her hands. So intense was her anguish that the bats that lived in the room's corners and beams squeaked and wailed, awake far earlier than usual. The carvings in the paneling were not only silent and still, but their little creatures were also hiding behind the carved wooden swags and bouquets.

"Oh, Marjory, what am I going to do? She'll destroy him. She'll make him *undead*. This was never supposed to happen. I went to Germany to get the Talisman, not–"

"Fight with vampires and other monsters and restore your ancestral home to its former splendor. Or as close as possible. You were a hero, my dear, a brave warrior. But we never know what's going to happen, Vanessa. We have to take what life gives us and roll with the punches."

"Lemonade out of lemons? I don't feel like dealing with platitudes now, Marjory. I've never lived life like it was a bumper sticker or a two-bit happy saying."

"You really love him, don't you?"

Vanessa's eyes flared, her ruff gave a spasmodic leap from her neck, and her wand filled her palm for an instant. Just as quickly, they retracted and her eyes filled. "Is it so obvious?"

"To me it is. You've loved him from the start."

Vanessa pulled a black hankie from her sleeve and dabbed her eyes. "It's so hopeless, Marjory. He's so *everything*… And I'm so terribly ugly. And a witch. An old witch. He'll never want me." She was silent a few moments, then implored her friend. "Do my feelings show so obviously? Does everyone know? Does *he* know?"

"I've known forever, Vanessa. But I know you very well. I expect that George Yeoman and most of the villagers know how you feel about Will Duane. They have magic of their own, and I'm a witch. You are far superior to me in rank, but I can intuit well enough. As can Cook and Driver, but we are like you. I don't think the people in your hospital here, the doctors and such, have any idea what you are. They certainly don't know about your feelings for… your dear friend. That's how the world sees you and Will. You are dear friends. Perhaps an odd couple, but the world has seen worse."

Vanessa covered her mouth with her hand. "Oh, Marjory. I suffer so."

Marjory could see her dear friend, employer, and superior in the order of witches struggling. She knew what Vanessa wanted to tell her: she'd gotten the talisman to charm Will somehow. But what she'd gotten in addition was to be ensnared in another witch's spell *and* the rules of their order, the inviolate code of witches. She'd returned with someone who not only could take Will from her, but could also destroy everything good about him. Vanessa could be forced to see Will marry another, *and* join the bloodsucking undead. Vanessa would never tell Marjorie any of this: she was as reluctant to talk about her feelings as she was to leave the estate.

"Vanessa, have you ever shared any of this with Will?"

"Oh, no, Marjory. I wouldn't dream of it. How could he possible care for me?"

"I think he cares for you very much, maybe not romantically, but as a person."

Vanessa snorted, "The old 'Let's be friends' ploy. The way you tell a boyfriend to get lost, 'without hurting him.' No, Marjory, I won't do that. I'll go ahead with what I've laid out for our little ghoul and let the chips fall where they may."

"I think you should talk to him. The words will come to you. If you really love Will, Vanessa, you'll help him avoid the vampire *and* stay true to the witch's code."

"How?"

"You'll figure it out."

7

LUNCH... & DINNER

This whole thing wasn't so bad. It was lonely, sort of, but after a few weeks, life found a rhythm. And she discovered a few ways to get kicks. That old goon, Mrs. Naughton, took her shopping to Stanford Shopping Center as promised. Having gone on sprees at the salons of the world's hottest designers, Adrianna could say that Stanford was OK. Just OK. The Naughton bitch arranged for a personal shopper for her, which Adrianna considered the minimum level of service acceptable.

The clothes she was allowed to purchase were appropriate for a sporty nun. Skirts and blouses, shorts and jeans. Tennis shoes, hiking shoes. A couple of dresses. They were expensive, their only grace. She was not allowed to purchase any evening wear or high heels. Nothing the slightest bit sexy. But she got the contact info for the personal shopper and pointed out a few things she liked on the racks.

"My aunt doesn't like me to dress like I am a woman," she whispered to the shopper, who whispered back that she'd be glad to work with her online, if she had a computer.

"You have an account in your own name." Oh. Not too bad.

Did she have a computer! When she complained about not having one, Naughton-babe came to her suite with a whopping new Numenon Ranger and all the accessories. Will Duane's company made them; Numenon made the best tech stuff in the world. She got her accounts going with the shops at Stanford and ordered some real clothes, then began stalking Will online.

That did not work; he had the tightest security she'd ever seen. Firewalls on top of firewalls. But she'd witch her way in soon enough. Mountains of information about Will existed online, plenty to occupy her. And images! Pages and pages. He was old, but gorgeous. He was shown with every supermodel and actress in the world. Adrianna had scowled when she saw that, but she'd have him to herself soon enough.

They signed her up for school, which was not so horrible, either. Adrianna was blessed to be both a witch and a vampire. Some of her vampire friends couldn't stay awake during the day. If they went into the sun, their skin blistered and they could go into convulsions and die. She could witch an impervious covering around herself and wasn't able to tell the difference between day and night, though she did have to wear sunglasses. *Mrs.* Naughton thought she had to take night classes, and signed her up for those, but Adrianna added a couple of day ones as well.

She was officially an interior design major, but got herself into pet grooming and animal care classes as well. Touching the animals and feeling their warm blood pulsating beneath her hands aroused her almost unbearably. Had she not discovered her little outlet by accident, Adrianna might have lost control.

But she didn't.

The beach was her saving grace. George Yeoman brought crates of animals over: squirrels, rabbits. Lizards. *Lizards!* Eggs with live embryos. A few deer, not many, and no fawns. A wild boar. She was expected to live on that crap, with an entire hotel full of upscale people available. But she did, going around stomach rumbling, sucking out the pathetic quantities of blood offered.

"George, do you know that a squirrel has less than half a cup of blood? That's not even a canape! Get me something bigger!"

He never did. That's when she discovered the really good part of the Ritz and the area around it: the beach. She could walk from Pacifica to Pescadero without anyone suspecting her. George Yeoman had his guards all over, of course, but what could she do out in the open in full view? Wearing ridiculous baggy shorts, a sun hat and huge sunglasses? Sometimes, she took a book and appeared to fall asleep while reading. Witching her watchers was easy: in days she had them staring at her apparent sleeping form while she was miles away, scouting.

The first one happened by accident. Long stretches of beach existed, interrupted by steep headlands and cliffs. Sometimes, boulders piled up, blocking the view of what was going on from anyone but those on helicopters or out at sea.

The dog was big, a mutt, and running scared. Just a stray. No one would notice that he was gone. He'd gotten himself trapped in an inlet and couldn't get around the rocks to get back to the main beach. The tide rose. He cried louder.

"Come on, sugar, I'll save you," she cooed. "Come on, baby." He wouldn't come near, cringing and holding his tail between his legs. "You stinking shit." Her hands shot out with her vampire's superhuman speed and strength.

He was delicious. She dragged his hull out to sea, washing her face and neck in the sea water. Easy peasy. And she'd never get caught.

She didn't, either, though the poodle was almost a problem. He was a standard poodle, reddish in color, very purebred. His owner was a middle-aged society babe, obviously so. She was with some guy, having a picnic on the beach. She let her dog run while she got it on with the guy. Younger guy, probably her personal trainer or something.

The poodle ran into the rocks where she waited. His blood was delicious. Adrianna thought that the delicacy and flavor of a dog's blood was directly proportional to how much it cost.

The lady was hysterical when she found the dog missing. She and her date ran around frantically screaming, *"Here Delacroix! Here Delly!"* Other people heard and joined the hunt.

Adrianna had to do a fast swim and rinse with the dead dog. Using her enormous strength, she shoved what was left of the curly corpse into the water far out of the cove. She swam after it, witching as hard as she could. Her friends came to her. When she saw three fins moving smoothly toward Delly's corpse, she screamed and swam in, being careful not to swim *too* fast.

"I saw him out there. He was swimming," she tearfully sputtered to the owner. "I tried to get him, but *they* came." Everyone could see the sleek gray forms rising from the water as they chowed down on Delacroix.

"Miss… I need to get some information for my report." The lifeguard approached her.

She was shooting up the beach, sobbing. Everyone thought she was too upset to talk, but Adrianna knew that no report of her hobby could ever be made.

Still, dog blood was not human blood. Lots of people wandered out the beach, climbing over rocks and seeking solitude. But she couldn't partake. Mostly, she couldn't get caught. A few days prior, Mrs. Naughton had relayed a message from Auntie Vanessa. "I know what you're doing. If you get caught, I'll project you back to Germany and cut you off. I found that in the witch's code: you will have betrayed my trust as I tried to fulfill my duty."

Germany did not appeal. California appealed. Surfing appealed. Mavericks appealed even more. Adrianna had never thought about surfing in her previous life. Wouldn't have considered it even now if the notorious Mavericks hadn't claimed another victim practically outside her suite's door.

Mavericks was a surfing destination about two miles from shore off of Pilar Point, which was a skip and a jump from the hotel. Because of the unusual formation of the sea's floor at that point, waves as big as any in the world broke at Mavericks. Big wave surfers, those suicidal maniacs, came from all over to risk their lives for cheap thrills.

Her nose told her where he was. Dead, but full of blood. He was drifting toward the Pilar Point Harbor when she found him. A two-mile swim was a piece of cake for her, but she didn't have to go out that far. She lost control with that feed; so much time had passed since she'd had proper food. She savaged him.

They thought it was a shark attack when they found him, so little was left.

Adrianna staggered into her room and collapsed in the vampire equivalent of a food coma.

She'd had no idea how dangerous living along the ocean was. Nor did the local population. Surfing accidents. Mavericks accidents. Drownings. Homeless people murdered as they tried to sleep on the beach. Adrianna fed only when she couldn't stand the hunger, when she almost was starved from subsisting on lost dogs and bunnies.

When was *Auntie* going to introduce her to Will Duane?

"You have been invited to a dinner party to celebrate the arrival of my cousin Adrianna Schierman at the Albion Club..." Adrianna leapt into the air when she came home from class to discover the formal invitation on the desk of her room. Vanessa was having a dinner at the fanciest, snobbiest country club in the West to introduce *her* to society. The old lady had added a note in her ancient, pointed hand-writing, *"Will has accepted his invitation. I hope to see you properly dressed and well-behaved."*

"Yes! Finally!"

8

VANESSA SPILLS THE BEANS

Vanessa paced around her laboratory, unable to concentrate on anything. Her experiments were stalled or untended; who could think of science at a time like this? Her lab occupied a three story addition she'd made to the mansion behind her rooms. No one new to the estate would know it was there, yet her lab would make the physics department of any major university proud. But today, nothing could calm her. Nothing *had* calmed her since the reports started coming in. Her hand grasped the talisman pinned to her dress. She wore it always.

"Vanessa, I must speak to you. *Now.*" Marjory's voice came through the intercom like a buzz saw.

"Why?"

"Look at your computer."

Vanessa turned to face the bank of large computer screens arranged in a two-level semicircle above her desk. "Oh my God!" She plopped in her computer chair, pulling up the local online newspapers and news blogs on other screens. All carried the story.

Four cattle had broken through a fence and run crazily over a cliff near Pescadero. No one had seen them do it, but a farmer's sharp action and fierce cow dogs prevented the rest of his herd from following.

"It was like they were in a trance," the stunned farmer said. He was shown in a work shirt, sitting on a tractor. "If it weren't for Flossie and Blue, I wouldn't have any cattle. They acted like they were under a spell, following the first batch. I've got them locked up, but they're banging against the corral walls, trying to get out."

The animals had run through the barbed wire fence, then galloped across the Coast Highway, over the headland, and off the cliff.

On one screen, a solemn newscaster stood with his back to the ocean. "The cattle apparently washed out to sea. The surf is rough and there's a vicious undertow here. There's no sign of them. We'll be reporting on this mysterious event as facts roll in. Another strange happening on the coast. Signing off, Kent…"

Vanessa shut off the report.

"It's her," she whispered. There'd been reports of dogs going missing up and down the shoreline from Half Moon Bay. Two fatal surfing accidents, one associated with a shark attack. Who knew how many homeless people sleeping on the beach had disappeared? Adrianna was doing it *while* being watched by George Yeoman's people. They had their own powers, but they weren't up to restraining the magick of a witch *and* vampire of the Schierman line.

"I've got to finish this," Vanessa said. She'd intended her dinner party with Will and a few friends—in addition to her bloodthirsty fiend of a ninth degree removed cousin—as a means to introduce the two and let Adrianna work her magic. She'd fulfill her part of the dreadful bargain.

She couldn't do it. But she had to do it. The witch's code demanded it; she had to be free of the bond Adrianna had put on her, and her spells. Vanessa had boasted to her young cousin that her magick couldn't touch her; she was too senior in rank. But Adrianna's spells could affect her, and had. She was bound to help that brat destroy the man she loved most in the world.

The code also bound her *not* to interfere with the workings and plans of the witch who held her in thrall. She was screwed, to put it the way most of the world would state the fact. Vanessa did not take to the condition, but she had no choice.

She had to protect Will. Vanessa's hands shook, growing colder than ever. Her finger joints stood out like knuckles on chicken legs. She had gone to Germany to fetch the talisman so that it could lure Will into loving her without him knowing. It would do that; she'd certainly spoken enough incantations over it since she'd had it, asking the amulet to procure Will's affection. (She asked, not demanded; one didn't command the Blood Talisman.) But now, if she was going to save Will, she'd have to use the jewel for something else.

She laid the talisman on her computer desk and held both hands over it, closing her eyes and entering a trance.

"O Talisman that carries my soul and blood, please watch over Will Duane. Save him. Don't let him be turned into a deathless monster. Take care of him the way I wish I could. Please. Send friends and spiritual powers to protect him. Do whatever is necessary. I can't stop Adrianna, but you can. I need your help."

Almost immediately, she got a transmission from the antiquity: To save Will, she had to give up the talisman. She had to give it to him.

"Oh, gladly. I'll do that gladly. I'll take it to him now." She charged back into the main part of the mansion, calling to Marjory. "Have Driver ready my Bentley! I must go to Will's." Then she started to cry.

Somehow, she found herself in the back of the Bentley with Marjory seated next to her.

"Everything will be all right, dear. You'll see." Marjory patted her arm.

Vanessa's brow knit. This familiarity with the staff was getting to be too much. Sometime earlier, she'd allowed Marjory to call her "dear." It was an emotional moment; she needed the endearment. Still, she'd chastised her housekeeper for overstepping her bounds. Marjory had responded that after all the time they'd been together and all they'd gone through, she had the right to call her "dear," whether she was her employer or not. Vanessa had grumbled, but in truth had liked the closeness.

Even so Vanessa hadn't invited her chief housekeeper to accompany her.

"Marjory, why are you here?"

"Because you need me, Vanessa. You are about to fall apart."

"I am not."

"Then why are you chewing on your finger?"

"What?" She was. She always did when stressed beyond bearing.

"What are we doing?"

"We're taking the talisman to Will. It's going to protect him instead of making him love me. It's a fair trade."

"Um, Vanessa, dear… have you called Will? Do you know if he's home? Or even in the United States? Does he know you're coming?"

"Oh, dear. I forgot." She closed her eyes to incant, then decided the cell phone in the car would be more appropriate. She pulled the awkward thing off of its stand. It was the size of a brick; state of the art for 1997. Hopefully cell phones would improve in the future. "I can't get a dial tone."

"It's all right. I called him before we left and told him we were coming."

Vanessa pulled herself up in indignation. "I didn't tell you to do that."

"Vanessa, I had to; you were incapable of coherent speech. Now, let's plan what you're going to say. You can't stumble into Will's house and start blathering about witches and vampires." She frowned. "You must get over your snobbery, Vanessa. You need people, and you need me. I am a witch after all. Accept my help."

"Isn't it beautiful?" Will glowed like a schoolgirl as he showed her his newly remodeled swimming pool. "I redid the decks with concrete stamped to look like river stone." Vanessa smiled for him through her anxiety. It was beautiful.

"Deciding to tile the pool's interior was a jump, but I think it was worth it, don't you?" He swept a hand toward the dazzling masterpiece.

The pool's bottom and sides had been covered with mosaic tiles—opalescent, mirrored, gilt, and colored glass. The design swept under the water from one end to the other and up the sides, sparkling in the sun.

The pool's bottom was a huge paisley, as tasteful as everything about Will.

"You taught me right, Vanessa! If you're going to do something, do it the best way and spare no expense." He peered into her face. "What's the matter? You look pale."

"Could I sit down and talk to you, Will? In private?" She felt faint. Wobbly.

"Yes. Can you walk? Do you need help?" Surprisingly, she nodded. Leaning on his arm was very comforting.

He took her to his private office, burrowed into his suite of rooms.

"This is as private as it gets, Vanessa. Wait a moment." He spoke into a mic on his desk. "All surveillance systems off." Then to her, "What's the matter?"

She looked up. Naked concern bathed his face. He was *worried* about *her*.

"I'm worried about you." She and Marjory had worked out a story. She was there because she suffered from anxiety. Worry. Old lady's nerves, that sort of thing. She was afraid of stalkers. She needed to give him something to quell her alarm. "I have a terrible fear of something bad happening to you."

"Yeah," he agreed, "so do I. You're talking about the patent infringement case. I thought it was a slam dunk in our favor, but it looks like the Supreme Court may see it differently. The decision should be announced next week." His expression was naked, baldly afraid. "I may lose everything. My money, my corporation. You know about the revolt at Numenon, don't you?"

She nodded. It was in all the papers. "Your board is turning against you."

"They have been for a long time. What happened at that retreat I went to in New Mexico last week really got them going. They think I'm a fruitcake. And now the patent suit is going south. I'll be out by the end of the year."

"Oh, Will, I'm so sorry."

He shrugged. "Easy come, easy go." Tears filled his eyes. "Except that none of it was easy." The tears spilled and ran down his face.

"Oh, Will, don't... Oh, here's my hankie." She pulled out a black lace-trimmed square. "I'm sorry. I didn't mean to come here to upset you."

"You haven't, Vanessa." He wiped his eyes. "I just..." He was crying! Really crying! She didn't know what to do for a moment, and then her motherly instincts took over. She moved next to him and put her arm around his shoulders. She certainly knew how to comfort children in pain. "Come over here." She guided him to the sofa and sat next to him.

"Will, we'll get through it. You have my support all the way. You don't even have to call me; I'll feel it if you need me and come down. You're bigger than those bullies in Numenon, Will. You're bigger and greater and more wonderful than your money."

That made him cry harder. Now his shoulders were shaking. His arms wrapped around her as he completely broke down and sobbed. "That's all right, dear. We'll get through it. I'll be with you."

They went on like that, ending with her whispering endearments into his hair and his tears coming to a slow halt. She sat next to him, not knowing what to do next.

Then he was embarrassed. "I'm so sorry, Vanessa. I didn't mean to do that..."

"Will, if you can't say how you really feel in front of me, who can you let loose with? We've known each other for forty years." Marjory had used those words with her, and they worked just as well with Will.

His chest heaved. "With all this hanging on me, I've been all bound up." He rubbed his breast bone with the heal of one hand. "I feel like shit, but I couldn't cry. Until now." He cried some more. "I might lose everything, Vanessa. Everything." He looked up at her, those brilliant blue eyes mesmerizing and in terrible pain. "Will you still love me if I'm not the richest man in the world? I'll love *you* no matter what."

"Of course, Will." What he said took a minute to sink in. He knew she loved him? He loved *her?*

"I mean that, Vanessa. I love you. No one has ever been as kind and caring toward me as you. Not my parents, or my ex-wife, or any of the w..."

Vanessa raised her hand. She didn't want to hear about Will's other *associations*.

"Anyone. That's why I can be who I really am with you. And show how I feel. I'm terrified, Vanessa. Money and success have been my life. And things that show that success. Like this house..." He glanced around at the vast modern architectural masterpiece of steel, glass, and granite, with modern art that belonged in museums on the walls. "What if I have to leave? Well, I have the Montana ranch..."

"Will, I understand what you're facing. I follow Numenon and you on the news, and I've been tracking that Supreme Court decision. It's serious, but I need to talk to about something else. Even more serious." She was supposed to say she had vague premonitions of danger. Something nebulous. "I have this feeling that you're being stalked by something really dangerous."

"I've been stalked by something or someone since I made my first billion." His face was tight.

"This is more than that. More supernatural..."

"You're talking about Enzo Donatore? The Spanish industrialist? Otherwise known as the devil incarnate? I know all about him. He tried to off me in New Mexico at that Native American retreat last week. Sucker failed big time. I've fought him and goons..."

Will's mood was turning angry fast. He spoke explosively. Vanessa knew all about Will's manic tendencies. Her chief psychiatrist had diagnosed him from her description of his behavior years ago. Having a mental hospital on the grounds was so handy.

"No, Will. Calm down. It's not the devil." *It's worse.*

"Well, I can handle him. Don't worry—"

"Will, it's worse than that. There's something you don't know about me. I'm a witch." Vanessa's eyes widened in horror. What had she done? She had no intention of ever telling him that.

"What?"

"I'm a witch. You know, *witch*. The ones with spells and incantations and mystical powers—though we don't wear pointed hats or fly on brooms. I can tell things that you can't. I can tell something bad from *my* realm is after you. Stalking you."

"Oh." Will rubbed his mouth, then raised his head to make eye contact. "That explains your house. And those creepy wall carvings. And the dogs. Everything."

"I like my house. I love my paneling!" Her chest heaved.

"That's fine, Vanessa. It's your house. But what is your realm and what are you afraid of?"

"My realm includes the worlds of magick and enchantment, which are very real, for your information. Not to be laughed at in the slightest. Spells, incantations, everything you've heard of witches. And it also includes everything supernatural, from angels to that Enzo Donatore. The devil. I know of him. My estate is protected by my angels; he can't come on it. Can't come near me, or it.

"I'm a White Witch, Will, just like you've heard about in fairy tales and bad novels for psychological adolescents. I exist to do good and make the world a better place. Everything in my domain serves the good of all humanity and all the other beings in existence.

"We are not *all* white witches, and witches, white or black, are not all of our world. It also includes orcs, trolls, ogres, and all sorts of monsters. Including zombies and vampires."

He looked at her. She'd lost him. "Don't worry about what I said. Just believe that I have special knowledge that makes me very worried about you. I came here to give you this," Vanessa pulled the Blood Talisman of off her bodice. "Takes this. You must wear it always."

Will examined the piece. "This is very old. It's beautiful. It must be very valuable. I can't take this from you." He started to extend his hand to give it back, but his hand froze.

"You can take it, and you will take it, and you will wear it until I tell you it's all right to remove it." She cast a spell when she spoke.

"Oh. OK. I'll wear it." He looked at the back. "It's got a pin on it. Too big for a tie tack though." Will grinned that glorious grin. "I'll get a chain for it." He put it on his desk.

"No you won't. I brought one." She pulled a gold chain from her pocket, threaded it through the eye on the back of the amulet and clasped it around Will's neck. "You will wear this always, and you will forget that I ordered you wear it. You will remember that you are in danger, being stalked, and you have to be careful." She snapped her fingers and looked at Will.

"Thank you, Vanessa. I really appreciate it. It's kind of big." The talisman was four inches across. "I'll wear it under my clothes when I'm out in public."

He kept studying her with his laser intensity. "You're a *witch*?" He shook his head with its beautiful silver-white hair and grinned at her. He'd always look like a delighted little boy. "I knew you were unusual, almost magical, but I never thought... I didn't believe witches existed."

"We exist, Will. I have a big family in Germany."

"The girl you're giving the party for tomorrow. She's your...?"

"Very distant cousin, yes. I reconnected with her on my recent trip to the mother castle. I went to get *that*." The talisman looked so beautiful on his chest. All he needed was chain mail and armor. Vanessa's happiness clouded over.

"What's the matter, Vanessa?"

"Oh, old-witch troubles, Will. Worried old witch."

"Don't worry about me, Vanessa. I fought off my board of directors and much worse. And I found something out in the desert at that retreat."

"What Will?"

"Uh, God. And a little old Native American holy man. And all sorts of things. Indian things. Kachinas and things." Will's mouth tightened.

"You can't talk about them."

He shook his head. "No. Insiders only. I'm protected, Vanessa, in a big way. And now by you." He stroked the amulet. "I'll be OK. Believe me."

Now *she* wept. She couldn't tell him that what searched for him was *worse* than the devil. He'd suffer thirst that only human blood could quench. He'd create others like himself just to survive. He'd leave all vestiges of his humanity behind. He'd be blind to love and light.

"Don't cry, Vanessa." Holding her in his arms, Will petted and whispered to her. "Nothing will happen to me. I'm very careful. I'm a canny old dog; I can sniff out danger. I've got your protection," he patted the amulet, "and I've got Grandfather's—that's the Native holy man—and his whole tradition. And I've got God, Vanessa." He seemed as embarrassed to admit that as she had been saying she was a witch.

She raised her head and looked at him. *He was holding her in his arms, just like she was a woman. And someone he cared for.*

"You know, Vanessa, people have said that I'm a warlock or something because of how things work out for me. Maybe I am, but I only have one skill: making money. I tend to fail at everything else." His face expressed all the loss in the universe. "Relationships, especially. You know that. Sometimes I wish that *we*..." She sat bolt upright. "...could have gotten together, but... our ages. We're so different. But I love you. I've loved you for a very long time." He kissed her forehead.

Vanessa couldn't move. She and Marjory had discussed truthfulness and admitting one's feelings. She had no idea it would lead to this.

"I love you, too, Will. I always have." She stroked the side of his head. It was impossible. She was ugly and old. He was beautiful. "But we're so different. I'm terribly private and opinionated."

"So am I. And controlling. I have to run everything. And I'm manic; I learned that at the retreat from a doctor. I take medication now."

"Why don't we just go on loving each other the way we are?"

Will melded into her, holding her to his chest. So tenderly, but so definitely. "You could have been the love of my life, if ..."

"I was fifty years younger."

"Shh." He held her close for a moment more. She felt as though she were melting, soft and feminine. Not like the bag of bones she actually was. Woozy and in love.

9

A DINNER PARTY

"All right, here we are." Vanessa directed Driver to pilot the car to the parking area nearest Adrianna's lair. The Ritz Carlton perched on the brow of the Pacific. Her eyes widened as she took in its majesty. The hotel was impressive even to one who was impressed by *nothing*. In the twilight, the hotel's low rise splendor stood out on the Pacific headland, its lighting accentuating the perfection of the five-star hotel.

"Let's survey the damage." Vanessa marched up the path to Adrianna's rooms with Marjory Naughton right behind. Both expected to see the ultra-posh suite shuttered to the light, splattered with blood, and littered with the bodies of dead creatures, hopefully not human.

Vanessa rang the bell. "Adrianna, it's Vanessa. We're at the door."

"Come in; it's unlocked. I'll be right there." Adrianna's voice came from the intercom.

Vanessa gingerly stepped across the threshold. The place was immaculate: the living room's wall of windows framed the Pacific Ocean. The setting sun died into the expanse of water, stirring and romantic. The suite was an open, lean spread of sofas and contemporary tables. She and Marjory walked around, ending in the small kitchen. No bloodstained knives littered the sink. But the place reeked of brimstone; the young witch had performed major magick to clean up her nest.

"It's nice to see what my money has been buying all these weeks," Vanessa sniffed. Marjory followed her out onto a wide deck facing the ocean. There it was: evidence of perfidy. A shaggy red cowhide rug was spread on the planks, dotted by chaise lounges and seating groups. The brand HC prominently appeared on what would have been the animal's hip.

"Do you recall the name of the rancher they interviewed on television?" she asked Marjory.

"Harold Crowder of the HC ranch." Marjory gaped.

"Our little friend is toying with us." Vanessa raised a hand, spat out a syllable, and the cowhide disappeared.

"Oh, hello, Auntie!" Adrianna stood in the doorway, radiant.

"I'm not your aunt, I'm your distant cousin." Vanessa's face was set and hard. "I'm sure that you're aware of what will happen if your escapades with surfers, dogs, and now cattle become public knowledge? Not only will you be in water hotter than you can imagine, your sins will come back to *me*. I will be suspect."

"Really, Cousin Vanessa? I never thought of that." Adrianna was round and appealing, her horrible paleness turned to rosy health. *Shows what the blood of four cows will do for a vampire,* Vanessa thought. The girl was dressed appropriately, in a demure mid-calf length gown. A very expensive gown; the personal shopper at Stanford Shopping Center had called for permission to charge it. "Will she look like a slut?" Vanessa had barked. The woman had been taken back, but assured that, "Miss Schierman will look the perfect lady."

And she did, a confection in pale lavender… which matched her eyes.

"I had to get contacts," Adrianna explained. "The light bothers my eyes; I have something called 'blue light sensitivity.' My contacts are tinted." Dark blue, making her bunny-rabbit-red orbs look violet. They were lovely with the dress. Adrianna was a tasteful, elegant vision. Vanessa's stomach churned. Would Will be able to resist her? Would any man?

"We'd better go. Will is always punctual."

"Oh, Cousin Vanessa, I didn't know you had anything like *this* in the garage." Adrianna went into raptures when she saw the car. Vanessa had

had Driver pull out the 1962 Rolls Royce Phantom V for their journey to the Club. She wasn't interested in creating a splash, though she knew the classic car would elicit it. Look what it was doing with the little Euro-tramp next to her.

Vanessa gave no significance to the trappings of wealth like the *arrivées récemment* cluttering up the Peninsula. No recently-arrived popinjays belonged to the Albion Club. The members were people whose wealth and standing were as longstanding as hers, or people like Will who, although he was richer than any of them, had the taste and manners not to flaunt it. The Rolls Phantom was simply the most comfortable vehicle to transport a vicious murderer to fulfill her fate with the man Vanessa loved.

They wound back the way they'd come on highway 92, moving from the open lands near the shore through cypress and pine forests. Just before they crossed the land bridge over Upper Crystal Springs Reservoir that would put them on I-280, they turned left. Most would never notice the small road through the trees; it had no street sign or marker of any sort. The meandering drive took them to the Albion Club, retreat of those beyond rich and famous. The spires of the Club's tall chimneys and a few rooftops could be seen from I-280, but other than that, the bastion of the upper crust was invisible.

Just the way she liked it. The Schiermans, along with the Crockers and Floods and a few other friends and robber barons, had founded the Albion shortly after the Gold Rush. It never changed, its dark green cypresses screening the building even from those who managed to find the road.

"Oh, my!" Adrianna squeaked when she saw its white stucco façade and low-dipping mansard roof. "It's like a French château."

"Yes, my ancestors and those of a few other eminent families put on the dog when they built this place. Wanted to grab the panache of the continent. I'd say they succeeded. Not that the continent has anything on the United States."

Adrianna's violet peepers widened as they approached the *porte cochere*. The building's roof extended over the driveway to allow at least four cars to disgorge their occupants without being touched by rain or inclement weather. The rest of the building would have done any of England's King Georges proud. Or the French Louies.

"It's like a fairytale. A real one." Adrianna appeared as delighted as a child and harmless as a fawn.

"It's considerably more pleasant than the family castle in Germany," Vanessa said sourly. "Let's get going." She led them into the familiar confines of the Club. Vanessa nodded at the doorman like a queen entering her realm.

"Hudson, you have my table prepared?" she said to the *maître d'hôtel*.

"Certainly, Dr. Schierman. Right this way." The dinner party was slated for a private dining room out of sight of the rest of the Club's members. Vanessa had set it up that way on purpose. What if Adrianna went berserk in such close proximity to Will and she had to subdue her?

The room was elegant, its high ceiling separating into arched segments ending with columns. They marked the walls, forming a circle around the dining table, which was a symphony of white linen and fine china.

"Are my other guests present?" she asked.

"Yes, Dr. Schierman. They are waiting in the lounge. They will be here directly."

Marjory Naughton squirmed uncomfortably. Vanessa had invited her to fill out the female roster. And also to have a friend close by. Vanessa was newly appreciative of the value of friendship.

"You look lovely, dear. Blue suits you," Vanessa reassured her friend. Marjory wore a tailored, full-length suit of blue slubbed silk and a matching hat with a small veil.

Vanessa had taken pains with her costume as well. She wore a dress of long, black *peau de soie*, a regal satin with a subtle sheen. She looked the way she always did, except for her sprightly brimmed hat with its long feather accent. *I'm a jaunty witch tonight,* she thought glumly.

Adrianna turned the heads of whomever saw her. She was a high-class mantrap.

"Well, here we are." Vanessa saluted the male guests as they walked through the arched doorway. "Good evening, Will. How do you do, Herman? And who do we have here?"

"This is Roland Raleigh, the young man who is making such a name for himself with our firm. I thought he and your niece," Vanessa bridled but didn't correct him, "might have something in common," Herman said.

Herman Compton was Vanessa's chief financial officer. He was recently single, again, and a good catch as a husband. She had not met Roland, but he was exactly what she had asked Herman to find for her: a young, very successful, beyond handsome young executive. Single. Vanessa did not intend to sacrifice Will without a fight. Given any luck, Roland should end up one of the wealthier people on the planet and as worthy a mate as any man. And he was in the prime of his life and looks.

Why not provide some menu options for the young vampire? The witch's code specified only that she provide Adrianna with *a* husband. Didn't have to be the one she indicated originally. Maybe the young hunk she'd seated next to her would turn her head. Or Herman. He was still good looking and worth a fortune.

"How do you do?" Adrianna extended her blood-plumped hand to Roland and spoke with her aristocratic and very slight German accent. He was almost dumbstruck. *Wonderful,* thought Vanessa. But Herman and Will were speechless as well.

The party rolled on, course after course, with no one really eating. She and Marjory couldn't eat due to nerves. Adrianna pushed her food from one corner of her plate to another; she never ate anything that wasn't alive and bleeding.

The men were too enthralled with Adrianna to pay attention to their filet mignon. They preened like fillies noticing a stallion for the first time. *Fools!* she thought. *You're acting like debutants at your first ball. You have no idea what you're courting.*

The conversation rose and fell around the table with excited, breathless tones. Everything Adrianna said was met with hilarious laughter.

Vanessa ordered extra wine and drank most of it. She had no idea how it was affecting her until she heard her voice bellow, "What do you mean, increase the Federal Reserve rate? The country's in a stall right now." Everyone stared at her; they had been discussing topics dear to the hearts of the financially involved.

"I don't think it's so much of a stall," Will said. "We've had deeper recessions, but you're right, anything could blow the bubble on the dot.com boom."

Things settled down after that. She felt embarrassed, but not too embarrassed, planning on switching to whiskey the minute she got home. God in heaven! Would this dinner never be over?

"I've had such a lovely time!" Adrianna cooed. "I never knew that discussing central financial markets and economic cycles could be so stimulating. But I have a midterm tomorrow. I need to get to bed." She batted her eyelashes the way Faline did in *Bambi* before the fire torched her.

"You're in *school?*" the three of them oohed. "What are you taking?"

"Interior design at Cañada College. I've got a drafting test tomorrow." *Bat. Bat* went the lashes. *Pitter patter* went their hearts.

You would have thought she said theoretical economics or quantum theory, Vanessa sniffed to herself.

"Oh, imagine that. I expect you're quite the talented designer," Herman said.

"I haven't done any real design to date, though I plan on redoing our castle in Germany when I go home."

The admirers duly noted that if she had a castle, she probably had the bucks to go with it and was therefore even more desirable.

"Do you do consultations? I just bought a condo in the city. I don't know what to do with it," added Roland. When she first saw the handsome Roland Raleigh, Vanessa had fantasized him as the legendary French hero Roland. He was the former Viking warrior who jumped ship and saved France, becoming immortal, though not the way Adrianna could do him up. Roland Raleigh was no fabled hero–*that* Roland had been smart.

"I'll have a brandy," Vanessa said. No one noticed, except the staff.

She was on her third brandy when Will, Roland, and Herman finished making appointments with Adrianna for free consultations. In house. Their houses. At night.

"I'm not a real designer, you know. I'm just beginning."

No matter; she could have been a chimney sweep and they would have booked her.

Vanessa slammed the brandy glass down. "Well, it's time for my beauty sleep. I'm exhausted."

"Oh, Auntie Vanessa, I'm sure someone can give me a ride home if you don't want to go all the way out to Half Moon Bay and back."

"You live in Half Moon Bay?" Roland said.

"Yes, at the Ritz Carlton."

"Why so far from Vanessa's house?" Will's hair was ruffled. He was ruffled. Also his cheeks were pink. Where was the damn talisman? Was it asleep at the wheel?

"Surfing. I live in Half Moon Bay for the surfing," Adrianna answered before Vanessa could say anything. "I just love surfing."

"*Really*," Roland gasped. "I went to the University of California in Santa Barbara as an undergraduate. It's right on the beach. I surfed every day. We'll have to go…"

"Yes, it's time to go. The Club is closing." It was, too; they'd been there innumerable hours. Vanessa raised her finger. The *maître d'* appeared. "Have Driver ready my car."

"I'll drive you home!" "I'll drive you." "No problem at all, Adrianna. It's practically in my neighborhood." Will was the most smitten of all.

Blood Talisman! What the hell *are you doing? You're supposed to protect this man!*

She stood up. "I'm taking her home. Where I come from, single men to not drive a young lady home the first time they meet her!"

Finally, they were home. Marjory gave her a little hug, looking worried.

"Vanessa, are you all right? You seem quite inebriated."

"No, I am not inebriated, yet. I intend to become inebriated right now." She made her way into the mammoth living room. The bats were well awake and trilled in greeting. "Go to sleep, Marjory, I can get drunk by myself."

And she did. How was she going to manage this? She had had no idea how attractive Adrianna could make herself. Now she did. Part of it was how the girl looked and acted; no member of royalty sitting on a throne could act as majestic as a penniless noblewoman in the market for a spouse. And her witching! She was a master. No one but another witch could tell what she was doing. She almost bewitched Vanessa.

"You can only have *one!*" she'd shouted at the little hussy when they were in the car. "One! I promised you one husband. The witch's code is satisfied by that. If you take them all, it's at your peril. I will come after you." Her ruff protruded fully and her wand shot out, burning a hole in Adrianna's dress over her heart. "If you touch more than one, I will not rest until I've put *you* in your grave."

"I don't know what you're saying, Auntie. I was just having a good time."

"I know all about your good time. If you *turn* any of those men during your 'interior design consultations,' you will marry him, dead or undead. Now get out."

Adrianna staggered up the walk to her room whimpering. *Good.*

"What am I to do?" Vanessa said to the empty space of the great hall. "Who will protect Will from that monster?"

"Why do you worry, Vanessa? Will is protected." She heard a soft man's voice that she'd recognize anywhere.

"Joseph? Joseph Bishop? Is that you?" Her dear old friend from graduate school at Berkeley in the 1930s. She had been in physics; he was getting a doctorate in divinity. A perfect pair. The new quantum theory dovetailed into his mysticism. He was the only Native American she'd known, an unforgettable character.

He sat in a huge wing chair on the other side of the room. His moccasin-clad feet came nowhere near the floor. His white braids hung lower than his belt, wrapped in fur and bead-trimmed. One tall feather stuck up above his head. Joseph's weathered brown face looked ancient, but it was the same face she'd loved for years.

"Joseph, I thought you were dead. It's been so long."

The old man grimaced. "People keep saying that, but as you can see," he held up his hands and arms, "I'm alive, regrettably. The Great One keeps bringing me back. This time for Will Duane. The last time was also for Will."

"You know Will?"

"Of course. I spent a week with him last week at my final retreat. He caused all sorts of trouble, and fixed it. Someone should tell you about it. Now, I'm here for you and Will. You need help."

"Yes, we do. The Blood Talisman isn't doing anything and… no one can stop her."

"How do you know that? Didn't you see us dinner? I was there, so were several others. We saw that she can charm anyone."

"I didn't know that. I couldn't see you. I'm so upset."

"You're drunk, too, Vanessa. A dangerous state for a witch. But I'm not here to lecture you. I'm here to tell you all is in good order. We see what you're up against, and so does the Great One. So get out of the way and let us work." He glared at her.

"Oh, please, Joseph, don't be angry with me. I'm just…"

"A greater witch than you can imagine. You'll see. Now go to bed and lay off the sauce."

When she awakened, sprawled in the wing chair in the living room, it was silent and empty. Joseph was gone. Will had met him at that retreat?

"Get out of the way and let us work," he'd said. Who? How?

Was that really him, or was it a drunken illusion?

10

A PRIVATE CONSULTATION

Vanessa paced around her room, distraught. The only time she had been this upset was when her husband, in a state of mania, stood on the roof in his straight-jacket, screaming that he could fly. The villagers built piled mattresses on the pathways below, hoping to cushion his fall.

But in his case, Heinrich was a warlock and *could* fly, which he did, zooming down the hill to his favorite pub in Woodside. His buddies took off his jacket and he had a high time of it until she tracked him down.

She didn't think this situation would turn out so well. Will was in grave peril. During the week since her dreadful dinner party, Adrianna had visited Herman Compton's mansion in Hillsborough and Roland Raleigh's San Francisco condominium. She knew this from the men, who had breathlessly called her about the marvelous ideas her protégée had for their homes.

"She's very talented, Vanessa," gushed Herman. "She had ideas my old designer couldn't imagine. I'm going to have her do the entire house."

"Don't get too involved, Herman. I don't know how long she'll be in the States."

"She said she's planning on being here for years." Her CFO sounded troubled. "She has to finish her schooling and she's thinking about setting up a design business here."

"Don't count on it, Herman."

Roland Raleigh was even worse. "We're going surfing on Sunday. I've got to find my board. Thank you, Dr. Schierman, for introducing us." He sounded euphoric.

"Watch out for sharks." What else could she say?

Adrianna hadn't savaged either of them, meaning she wanted Will. No mystery; Vanessa had known whom she wanted from the start. It was Saturday night; party time for most of the planet. The night when witches howled and vampires supped and the rest of the population celebrated.

Will was having dinner with the Beast in his penthouse atop the Numenon Building. The Beast was a far better name for the little slutty bloodsucker than her upper class appellation, Adrianna. Vanessa wanted to gouge out her eyes.

"Stop it! That isn't you! You aren't an evil witch." She went back to pacing. Strangely, on this night that Will might be turned into a soulless monster, she'd taken pains with her dress. Or undress. Vanessa wore her white cotton batiste nightgown trimmed with fine lace and embroidered pink flowers. The gown was the only truly feminine thing she owned. Over that she'd donned a royal purple silk velvet robe with satin lapels. She took her hair down and wore it in a long braid.

She'd dressed like a bride—for a funeral.

"Oh, I can't stand this." She dialed Will's cell phone again, not leaving a message. She'd already left five. She couldn't let this happen.

"Blood Talisman! What are you doing? You're failing me."

If the talisman was working, the stinking bloodsucker should have detonated in the car on the way to his condo. It should be all over the news. *"Woman explodes in Lexus."* She checked the TV in her room. It wasn't. Was it too soon to call him again?

Vanessa whirled, beginning another circuit of her room. A knock at the door interrupted her furious progress.

"I brought you a milk drink," Marjory said, entering without permission.

"I didn't ask for one. And how do you know how to make my drinks?"

"You didn't ask for one, but you need a milk drink. I've watched you make these for eons, Vanessa. And this is one of *my* drinks, not yours.

Down the hatch." Marjory stood watching until Vanessa consumed the whole thing.

"Hmm. Tastes slightly different than mine."

"Of course. Every witch has her own formula. Yours would put a bull elephant in rut to sleep. Mine is slightly different. Now get in bed."

Marjory tucked her in and kissed her forehead. Vanessa was profoundly embarrassed and equally grateful. "Thank you, my dear friend."

"Go to sleep, Vanessa. When you awaken, it will all be over, one way or another."

The effect of Marjory's milk drink was *much* different than hers. Vanessa felt herself drifting off, happy and content, but where she went wasn't the oblivion of slumber. She felt herself expand, widen, and move.

She was in Will's penthouse condo in San Francisco. It was an urban paradise meant for seduction, which is what Will used the place for; she knew his predilections very well. He brought his fancy women here. The views from the top floor of the Numenon Building, the tallest in San Francisco, were stunning. Vanessa hoped that Will had heeded her admonitions about earthquake safety while building the skyscraper. *She* remembered what happened in 1906, even if those silly public officials and architects didn't. A building that high situated practically on the San Andreas Fault was insane. But there it was, and the glitter of San Francisco's lights from its crown would melt the reserve of any woman.

Marjory's milk drink had a strange effect: Vanesa was in Will's condo, yes. But she *was* Will's condo: the walls furniture, artwork, air. Everything. She *inhabited it*, as though she was it. Being a leather sofa was an odd sensation, but she would definitely know what was going on, if anything went on. Adrianna wasn't there.

I've always wanted to be a fly on the wall, thought Vanessa. *Now I am,* and *the wall.* And the people. She was inside Will and could hear him thinking.

Adrianna, the Buzzard (an epithet almost as good as the Beast) was keeping him waiting.

Vanessa smiled. Will *hated* lateness, especially from "dates." He also had a horrible temper when insulted. *Will Arianna get a big surprise if she arrives one second later? She'll find out that the rumors about his temper understate the actuality. She'll be lucky if he doesn't bite* her. Vanessa smiled, feeling as though the entire apartment grinned with her. It did. Fortunately, nothing showed.

Will scowled and looked at his watch. He was dressed for seduction, wearing a black satin smoking jacket with trousers sporting satin stripes down the sides. *Rather overdone, Will. You're presuming a lot, my dear.* She chuckled silently. She thought it was funny! She was laughing in the face of Will's demise.

DING! DONG! The doorbell chimes reverberated through her. Shocking sensation. She hoped not too many people were invited to the soiree. She vibrated with the bell.

"I'm sorry I'm so late, Will. I drove myself. You drive on the right side of the road here, like Germany, but there were so many signs I couldn't figure out." Adrianna arrived breathless and resplendent in lavender and her charming accent.

He stood stiffly, mouth compressed. But he wanted to smile and forgive her, Vanessa could tell. Oh dear. Her witching was powerful. Oh dear again. Will helped her out of a long lavender velvet cape, hooded like Cinderella's. Or the big bad wolf's.

Lord in heaven! All the furniture jerked when it saw her dress. This was what Vanessa had been afraid of at the dinner party. Adrianna wore a collection of sheer silk panels, hankies, really, that barely covered *anything*. Her hard nipples were inches from Will's hands as he took the cloak. His fingers trembled. Vanessa could *smell* her brimstone, yes, but mostly pure female hormones and lust. Will was done for.

"So, you want to talk about interior design. What do you think of this?" Will straightened and stood stiffly, sweeping an arm toward the condo's open living area. The city lights almost overwhelmed Vanessa, and she'd already seen the view.

"Oh. You don't really need décor with this view, do you?" whispered Adrianna.

"No, but I have it anyway. Look around."

Perfect. Perfection upon perfection. Beauty speaking beauty until there was nothing left to be said. The space could not be improved.

"Oh." The vamp was silenced.

Will turned on her. "Why are you here, Adrianna?" He faced her, glaring. "What do you want?"

"I just… want to be friends."

"No you don't. You would have come to my office for lunch if that's what you wanted. Why are you here, in the night, dressed like a high-priced hooker?"

She backed off. Vanessa could feel her straining not to lose control. "This is a *Vitienne*. It cost a whole month's allowance."

"Sorry, honey, you wasted your money. I'm immune."

"What? What are you saying?" she sounded genuinely aggrieved, but Vanessa could sense Adrianna was straining not to attack.

"Want to play 'What no one knows about Will Duane'?" he spat out the words.

"Of course. I love to play–"

"No, you don't. You love to hurt. What you don't know about me *Ad*-rianna is that my father turned me on to hookers when I was fifteen."

"What? That's…"

"Pretty shitty, but it knocked the dummy out of me. I can see a whore a mile away. I smell them. You are the biggest twat for hire on this continent. You will get nothing from me." His teeth clacked together. His ribs pumped. His next volley of words rocked everything in the condo back.

"What did you do to Vanessa? You've got her scared stiff."

Being able to feel the feelings of all the actors in the play was not pleasant. Will was so angry that Vanessa thought he'd tear Adrianna to pieces. She was just as angry, but also surprised.

"Oh, *Auntie* Vanessa." Adrianna's stance changed like mercury. "My dear auntie…"

"She's not your aunt. I'm surprised that you're any relation at all. What hold do you have on her?"

Adrianna's fangs started to drop. "She owes me. It's a matter of honor, and our law."

"Your law. You're a witch, too."

Adrianna smiled and inched closer to him.

Be careful, Will! Vanessa's soul cried. Adrianna reached out a manicured hand, as though wanting to stroke the back of his head.

"Get away from me, you bitch. You are so obvious." He laughed at her. Laughed in her face. "Don't you think I've been up against your kind before? I've had demons here, in this room, trying to kill me. Punching me, fighting with me. I almost killed one, right there," he added proudly with a jab toward the cocktail table. "You think I'm afraid of you? Last week, your boss, Enzo Donatore... know him?"

Vanessa could tell that Adrianna didn't, but she'd find him as soon as she could.

"Enzo and I went *mano a mano* all over the New Mexico desert. He and all his goons couldn't kill me. Do you know why? *Do you know why?*"

Adrianna backed off, overcome by the force of his words. But that wouldn't hold her off for long. Vanessa shrieked a silent warning to Will. All the furniture jumped and the paintings wiggled on the walls. *Run, Will. Run for your life.*

Will appraised his opponent. "So you're not Donatore's. Whose are you, bitch?" Will spit the words in her face. "Tell me who sent you and release Vanessa. Then I'll let you live."

Adrianna flipped at that. "*You'll* let *me* live, you foolish mortal. *I am eternal.* I will live forever. You will be mine *now.*" Adrianna hissed. Her clawed hands rose and her blood red eyes almost exploded in their sockets. Fangs glinted even in the room's dimmed light. Adrianna's ruff, fine German lace, shot from her neck and her etched silver wand deployed. She was a witch and a vampire!

Adrianna leapt at Will, screaming.

Then jumped back in terror, hands shielding her face. "No! No!" She fell on the floor. And disappeared.

Will stared at the space where she'd been. "Adrianna?" He looked around as though she might be hiding. "She's *gone.*" Will staggered backward and flopped on the couch.

Ooph, Vanessa huffed on the receiving end of the couch. He was heavier than he seemed. But now she could feel Will and the couch and something he was digging for in his smoking jacket. He pulled out a soft leather pouch, beaded and fringed and hanging from his neck by a thong. He sat for a moment, catching his breath, and then pulled the leather ties that closed the pouch. He pulled the Blood Talisman out and held it in his hand.

"Oh, Vanessa. Thank you. I didn't tell her that when I fought the demons and Enzo Donatore, I had the aid of God and all the angels and most of the Native American deities." He held the talisman to his chest and dropped his head in prayer.

"You had more than that, Will Duane," a soft voice remarked.

"Grandfather! What are you doing here?" Will sat erect, still clutching the amulet.

"The same thing that amulet is, saving your hide. What I did in the Mogollon Bowl, or rather what the Great One and all the Ancestors and spiritual beings did. You didn't think you could face that monster alone, did you?"

"No. Well, I did at the time, but I think I—"

"Underestimated that job. Happens so often. But at least you could tell she was a trap."

"Yes. From the instant I saw her. Even heard about her. Vanessa was so worried about me. It broke my heart that she was so upset. I wanted to kill that—"

"I believe you did kill her. Or will. But…"

"Grandfather, would you materialize?" Will spoke into space. Vanessa could see no sign of her old friend in the room. "I can't see you? Where are you?" Will looked around the room frantically.

"Oh, certainly." The tiny American Indian holy man stood in the middle of the room in his moccasins and feathers. War paint covered his face. A ten-foot-tall primitive crucifix leaned against his shoulder. "I thought it was my paint that scared her off, but I think it was this." The crucifix was made of whole logs, decorated and carved by an aboriginal artist. The depiction of Christ on the cross was agonized, each lash and wound dripping with painted blood.

"That is grizzly," Will said.

"Yes, effective. The vampire ran screaming when she saw this. I borrowed it from the Cathedral in Santa Fe. It's the one in that alcove; I'd better return it." He started to fade.

"Wait, please. I need to talk to you. Vanessa and I have become very dear during this incident. Is she free of whatever hold Adrianna had on her now?"

"Oh, yes, though she will be even freer still soon."

"I love her, Grandfather." Vanessa, whose soul inhabited the entire apartment, but especially the couch where Will sat, almost swooned. "I've often thought that we should... I don't know, marry or something."

"Well, I think 'or something' will have to do. For now, Will. I can't say what will happen in the distant future, but what I have been given to see shows your life moving in a different direction. You will live many years, Will Duane; who can say what turns your life will take?" He was fading. "I must go. This crucifix is very heavy. But wait here. This evening is not over yet."

Good God in heaven, thought Vanessa. *What else could happen?*

The phone rang. Will moved slowly, as if in a dream. He picked up the phone.

"Elizabeth! How are you?" Will came to life in a jiffy. "You're calling from your family's ranch in Oregon? What a surprise... after you left the retreat last week, I didn't think I'd hear from you again." He was delighted, amazed. Vanessa had no idea who Elizabeth was, but she hated her.

"Oh. Yes, I meant what I said at the retreat. I can have a plane pick you up next Saturday at your ranch's landing strip. We'll do dinner at my house. Maybe I'll fly with my pilot. I'll see you... sooner."

Vanessa's incorporeal jaw dropped. He was making a date with another woman! Someone he was genuinely glad to hear from. *Amulet,* she intoned to the jewel, *find out who she is.*

Will got off the phone beaming. He went over to a credenza and picked up a magazine. *People Magazine's* "Woman of the Year Issue." Who Elizabeth was became clear right away: her picture was on the cover. Elizabeth Bright Eagle, MD, MPH, the *People Magazine* 1997 Woman of the Year.

Vanessa looked over his shoulder, or rather through his shoulder and eyes, as he read the article again. The issue was well-leafed, having been read many times. She was a Native American, tall and with impeccable posture. The look of a warrior shone from her eyes. She was beautiful, uncompromising, and powerful. Not one of Will's chippies at all.

As Will flipped pages, Vanessa could see Elizabeth in her various roles: medical doctor, lecturer, researcher, political activist. Horsewoman. Expert markswoman. She was everything: brilliant and brave and strong.

Vanessa was delighted to see that she'd eaten more than her share of the pork chops. The woman was heavy, but beautiful. Someone who was Will's match. He was in love with her. Vanessa's heart sank as she realized it.

She thought the vampire was it; get rid of that menace and Will would be hers. But it wasn't to be. He would pick up Elizabeth Bright Eagle at her family's ranch in a week, and they would begin a flight of their own.

Vanessa was in her own bed, tears running down her face. He loved her, she knew that, but he wasn't to be hers. Now.

She knew she would live many, many years. Perhaps some of them included Will and her. Perhaps.

She heard Grandfather's voice: *"Who can say what turns your life will take?"*

No one could. Her life wasn't so lonely. She had the estate to run, and the hospital with her children, and the village. All the folk she'd adopted and made her own. And her fortune to manage. Vanessa wasn't alone.

"Please God," she whispered, "if you can see to it one day…"

Hovering between wakefulness and sleep, Vanessa heard Marjory's voice, "Vanessa, dear, do you know how old your mother was when she died?"

"Huh? What? I don't know."

"She was 278 years old."

"She couldn't have been that old."

"Ophelia Schierman was 278 years old."

"She looked beautiful in the crypt."

"Yes. How many women look beautiful years after they've been laid in a crypt?"

Vanessa sat up, wide awake. Marjory wasn't in the room; she was witching nearby. "What are you saying?"

"Your mother used her witching skills on her appearance. She was never a natural beauty; she made herself what she was using her magick. She kept herself beautiful the same way, though long dead."

"Why are you telling me this?"

"Darling, no one lives forever. You'll outlast that Elizabeth person, and you can keep Will going, too. He has the Blood Talisman, remember. It will protect him. And Vanessa, witches don't need nips and tucks to keep up our appearances, we just need a little… sparkle from a wand. Just a little, though. You'd never guess how old I am."

Vanessa sat thinking. *Mother used magick to be beautiful?* The realization stunned her. *She was a fake. I knew she was a fake, but I didn't realize her* face *was fake.* After a moment's consideration, *I could do that, I just never thought of it. I wouldn't do anything flamboyant or flashy. I would make myself a handsome woman, but not so good-looking as to be vulgar.*

If I made myself better looking and younger, Will would notice me. He said he loved me even looking as I do. If I used magick to transform myself, I wouldn't have to use my time machine. I would remember everything that's happened in my life, and I'd look good enough to attract Will.

I can get what I want. Eventually. I can wait.

She fell back to sleep, a smile on her face, until a thought intruded: *I wonder what happened to Adrianna?* She was free of the bond the other witch had put on her, but what had happened to her adversary?

11

THE SECOND TIME AROUND

Adrianna clawed her way through pitch blackness. Wherever she was, whatever she was running through, grabbed at her. If she stopped, she'd be frozen in stone. Her breath rattled in her throat, each gasp more ragged than the one before it. Screams surrounded her. Shrieks. Howls. *Her* screams.

At last, Adrianna pulled herself out of the rock, falling into an open space. The area was pitch black, offering no way to navigate the darkness. But at least nothing clutched at her or tried to trap her. She could stop and think for a moment.

What had happened?

She was about to make Will Duane her husband and lover and slave, when something jumped between them. Thinking of it propelled her feet and legs. She was running again, arms outstretched, sobbing.

A face had appeared right before her. A horrible face. A gargoyle, a monster. At first, she could only make out pieces: dark wrinkled skin, beady black eyes. A feather sticking up. Amulets in bags stinking to hell. The face! Crumpled in a smile, a kind smile.

Leave here, demon! Be gone! That's what he said, but it was in another language. He was an Indian, the first she'd seen.

He held a huge statue up to her. It repelled her like nothing she could imagine. Cousin Vanessa's wand had become a cross when she killed Laurenz so long ago. But that was nothing compared to this monstrosity. The crucifix was wood, *wood*, the enemy of vampires. Its face was a visage of pure suffering. Painted wounds covered the figure on the cross, dripping blood. This wasn't delicious, wonderful blood, but blood that hurt and reminded her that hurting others was evil. She was evil. The giant cross that the horrible little Indian waved at her would kill her.

She instantly projected out of the condominium.

But where? Where was she? Adrianna slowed to a walk, feeling for some way of orienting herself. It came when she'd gone as far as her legs would carry her. She staggered when she heard it.

Eerie wailing surrounded her. Carved stone walls, each slab carefully fashioned and placed, became visible. Arched columns reached up to vaulted ceilings. She was in the catacombs below the castle, *her* castle. She was home in Germany! A gasp of joy escaped Adrianna's lips. She was under the castle somewhere, in her ancestors' tomb. She was with her people, though they had been witches and not vampires like her. But that was an accident. She hadn't meant to become one of the undead and feel their terrible thirst.

"Please forgive me! I didn't mean to! It was a big party—I know you've been to big parties and gotten carried away. You've done things you didn't intend to do. I'm sorry. If you could forgive me and let me go back to being a witch, I'd do anything.

"I'll change. I won't be lazy. I won't lie or spend all our money. I'm *sorry! Please forgive me!*"

Adrianna had no idea if anyone heard. Can the dead hear? Probably not. She kept walking. Pillars and rectangular stone crypts provided some measure of the hall's length. Each stone bore a name. Very important people had their places of eternal rest commemorated with statues. Some had alcoves or whole rooms carved out of the rock. She walked faster, seeing engraved names, all bearing the surname Schierman.

The catacomb had no exit and no entrance. Just corridor after corridor lined with stone blocks, each the resting place of a relation. Endless, just like eternity.

When she realized the maze had no way out, Adrianna wept. She had lost. *I didn't mean to become a vampire. If I could go back, I wouldn't do it. I want to be a witch. Please forgive me. Let me out of here.*

No answer. Except light. Motes of light came from somewhere, illuminating her steps and pointing her toward a grotto, the largest sepulcher she'd seen. An elaborately carved granite block rested in the middle, lights playing around it. A crystal cover, like the top of a coffin, was opened along the long side of the block. No one lay there; the tomb was waiting for someone.

Her.

Adrianna screamed and tried to run, but couldn't.

You said you wanted a second chance. You'd do anything to have it. Did you mean that? Or do you want to wander down here for all time? Do you want to feel your thirst for blood and have no way of slaking it? Be a ravenous vampire forever?

She recognized the voice from somewhere, but she couldn't say where. "No! I don't want to be locked up here. I don't want to feel like I do. I want to be a witch again."

Good.

Something shoved her toward the granite slab. Adrianna fought, but to no avail. As she slid toward the open coffin, the faces and names of all the people and animals she'd "changed" came to her. People at parties all over Europe. Servants from the castle. A man on an airplane. Surfers and derelicts on the beach. Dogs. Cattle. Their death cries assaulted her.

"No! No! I'm sorry." But she fought on.

Adrianna ended up on her back on the stone slab, legs outstretched, hands crossed on her chest.

Move your hands farther down, Adrianna.

She did and something struck her. Passed through her, destroyed her. Her eyes opened as she lay dying. The top of the crucifix emerged from her chest. She could see the agonized figure on the oaken cross, the crown of thorns, the nails in his hands. The piece was beautifully rendered: a masterpiece of religious art had pierced her heart and killed her.

I knew you'd appreciate this crucifix. You have excellent taste.

The dead Adrianna saw the cold face of Vanessa's mother hovering over her. The crystal cover to the sarcophagus closed, sealing her in.

You should thank me, little girl. You're no longer a vampire. You'll rest here a while. As long as I say, and then you'll return to the world, as I am going to do right now. I've served my time with the dead.

Adrianna could see Ophelia Schierman in all her glory, alive and radiant, standing next to the coffin.

"Witches *can* live forever, Adrianna. People just don't know about it. It's part of our code. We spend a little time in death to atone for our *sins*, our naughtiness, and it's back in action.

"I suffered so much when I was married. Heinrich thought he was so wonderful, the blood in his veins noble and pure. He considered me a bit of Euro-trash and rubbed it in every chance he got. Until I killed him. *You*, with all your ancient ancestors, were insistent on making yourself trash. I trust that my daughter has taught you some manners."

Adrianna tried to nod her head and say, *"Yes!"* But she was dead.

"I'll take that as a yes. And I'll tell you what I have planned for you. I will take control of the castle and the European Schierman clan. I can do it better than the remaining dissolute roués and hangers-on. When I've restored our fortune, I'll restore you to life and find you a husband worthy of you.

"Vanessa has always disappointed me. Too ugly, too smart, and too stupid to realize she could use magick on herself and make herself look however she wanted. She could transform her pathetic children and husband into normal people. She could have everything.

"All Vanessa had to do was take a trip on the dark side.

"Black magic isn't so wrong, Adrianna. I know *you* realize that. That's why I'm adopting you. When you've done your time in the casket, you'll be my daughter, and my right hand. *We'll* show the world the power of the Schierman name." She chuckled. "You're beautiful. You have no morals and extremely powerful witchery. *You* are the daughter I wanted and deserved. So sleep. I'll awaken you when your penance is through."

Tears of joy ran down the sides of Adrianna's face, but she lay still and cold.

"It's the witch's code, my darling. We can't always get what we want on the first go round, but nothing can stop us on the second." Ophelia's beautiful head cocked to the side as though listening.

"Oh, my dear. Don't worry about Will Duane. He's always been mine. I will take him when the time is right. No one—especially my daughter—can do a thing about it."

Adrianna watched the older witch move gracefully from the tomb. Ophelia Schierman was an exquisite, elegant lady. She wore a slender black sheath, her flamboyant sparkles and gaudy lights gone. The second time around, she'd get it right.

HOW
DID YOU BECOME
A WITCH?

"You're either a witch,
or you're not."
Vanessa Schierman PhD

THREE

How Did You Become a Witch?

THE SCHIERMAN ESTATE

"How did you become a witch? That's the stupidest question I've ever heard." Vanessa Schierman sat in the gloomy great hall of her mansion, speaking into a shiny little device with a black glass front and chrome edges.

"You either *are* a witch or you're not." She shouted the words into the microphone with gleeful indignation.

"You know you're a witch when your ruff leaps from your neck, its jeweled spines shooting venom, your wand leaps into your hand—and people fall dead. Or something. First spells are often erratic.

"I was three when it happened to me." She fiddled with the shiny recorder and set it on the little oak table with its twisted, barleycorn legs. "iPhone. Whatever idiot designed that probably made a fortune." She lifted her cut crystal glass and took a healthy swig of amber liquid.

She continued to ruminate, getting closer to the source of her irritation as she did. "I don't know why I let that writer person into my life, much less my house. The beginning was so innocent: Cook saw her note on the bulletin board in the Village. The writer had perfect penmanship and the message was properly spelled and in good English. That was the first thing that attracted me. So few speak the language any more. And it was on our town board; no one would sneak in and post on *our* board.

"The whole thing seemed harmless: the card said its writer was doing research and wanted to talk to a real witch—that was the hook for me. As a research physicist, I have a natural fondness for those who do research instead of just making things up.

"I looked her up on that infernal Internet that rules everything these days. The *author* had written lots of books with compelling covers and had stellar reviews. I told my secretary to contact her, and soon I found myself invited to tea at her home."

Vanessa could remember day as though she was living it. Driver made his way down through the redwoods to the flats. He pulled into a U-shaped driveway in a modest, but not squalid, neighborhood. She sniffed and surveyed her destination through her car's window. The author's house was plain and dated, but well kept.

Most importantly, she lived in Woodside. Vanessa's estate topped the mountain and extended forever. The author's place filled a notch in a gully far below, but within the town limits. That was acceptable. For heaven's sake, portable toilets go for millions as fixer-uppers in Woodside. One must accept all economic levels.

Vivid flowers flowed up the curved walkway to the house. Vanessa was used to the fog swathing the mountains above the town, but the sun had a certain appeal. And the house looked charming up close.

Who could see the harm in what she did? The author herself was at least presentable. She had the manners Vanessa demanded in her kitchen maids and spoke better than that. She said was looking for an "authentic voice" for a witch in something she was writing—and look what happened.

Vanessa carried her standard nondisclosure contract; making it clear that whatever she said would be for background material only. The author would not quote her, reveal her identity in any way, or publish what she said *anywhere* without written permission. The author signed it. The agreement was legally binding.

That and the author's demeanor fooled Vanessa into feeling she was safe. The woman listened without any questions, interruptions, or judgments. Vanessa ended up prattling away.

"We've been living here on the estate for hundreds of years, our ancestors coming from Germany … well, before any other Europeans. We've always been industrious, so of course, we did very well."

Vanessa found herself saying more than she should have about the family and life. So much so that she began to think that the *writer* was a witch who charmed it out of her.

The relationship went from a visit or two at the woman's home in the gully to her visiting Vanessa's estate. She loved the estate, which proved she was a witch; most people fainted when they saw Vanessa's home.

The dismal fog, baying dogs, turrets poking out of the mist, as well as the grotesque carvings on the exterior had regrettable effects on most guests. Also, the carvings on the walls inside and out moved. They couldn't resist wiggling for new guests. The cavorting bas-reliefs loved to watch visitors run for the door.

But this woman, this *enchantress,* loved it and got Vanessa to talk more. She spoke about her husband and children, and personal disasters of the most painful kind.

She said, "My husband and I were such a mistake. I met him during my year on the continent. I wasn't so homely then. Grew into a swan for a while, until I fell off that horse and this happened." She sighed, trying to straighten her head and neck. Hopeless. The bones were fused. "I was a handsome woman, tall and comely. Rich, with an ancient German family, though our branch had emigrated to the United States hundreds of years ago."

She had told the author all of this, and shared her tender feelings for her spouse and how it all went wrong when they discovered that they were very distant cousins and bore the same genetic flaw. "Of all the inherited scofflaws possible, ours was the worst. Our five children ... so ill. And then, finding him hanging there when his depression took over."

From that, Vanessa found herself where she was. It was to be an interview or two. Background material. But here she was, months later, spilling her guts into an electronic device. "Just say a few words into a recorder," author creature cajoled. "I'll have them transcribed. Your children will have a record."

Vanessa had suspected the writer wanted material to make into a book all along. She wanted her secrets! And she had them. But Vanessa had her contract and its flimsy legal protection. She had more than that—the *author* had told her of on-line trolls lurking on the Internet waiting to attack hapless and innocent writers. Vanessa had *real* trolls living in the forest behind the mansion. How would Ms. Author like a visit from those, in addition to her attorneys?

The old witch cackled, or maybe it was the Scotch roughening her voice. The idea of the author person running from a real troll delighted the old lady. Those rocklike, hairy things would love author meat.

She looked around the huge hall, with its lead-paned windows and marvelously ornate, dark furniture. Tapestries covering the walls depicted her ancestors in the old country, hunting game and run-away peasants. Homey and warm scenes of rape and pillage. It would have been a perfect evening at home, except that the carved wood paneling was quiet, not a gnome or beastie wiggling across its face. She *liked* their cheery addition in the manse.

"Wake up! I've sold you out, you little bastards! Done everything but put it on the TV!" She yelled at them, tilting the decanter and refilling her glass.

"That writer person wants to know how I became a witch. Don't you want to be part of the tale?" Vanessa looked around the room, shadows impenetrable as the light waned, resident bats stirring in the beams. The wood paneling gave a heartening hiccup and nasty little creatures peeked from between the seams.

"How could I *not* be a witch, born *here* from *my* parents?" She picked up the device and hit "Record." Her voice barked out now, loud enough to fill the hall's corners and crevasses, and awaken any lingering dead.

"It happened when I was three. My parents were in the kitchen, having a row. They'd been having a row all my life, variations on the theme.

"'She's not mine,' were the first words I recall, shortly after I emerged from between my mother's legs. I was greasy and covered with fluids and quite unable to object. My father leaned over me and said, 'She's not mine! She belongs to that Viscount, What's His Name.'

"'Of course she's yours, Heinrich. Only you could sire such an ugly baby.'

"Those were the first words I heard. I understood them perfectly, of course; it's a facility we Schiermans have. They shaped my life.

"I grew from an ugly baby to a tall, gangling toddler whose elbows and knees seemed to multiply if anyone looked at me. I was horribly shy and stuttered. Not a good representation of the family line.

"My mother put me on a horse early, saying, 'It's so dangerous. She'll be forced to develop balance and poise or be killed.' My death seemed a constant refrain with them.

"And so we ratcheted forward, a family of sorts. Him screaming about my mother's infidelities; her screaming about his. The bats flapped through the mansion and the servants stalked about with funereal faces, even though no one was to die for years.

"I took it for three years before putting a stop to it. On that fateful day, *my birthday*, things got out of hand. My parents threw a big party for me. All the villagers were invited and came, though through the rear entrance only, of course. I didn't realize at that time that not everyone had a village of primitive retainers living in the woods behind the house. They were so useful, cleaning up, building things, and so on.

"And did Cook bake me a treat! An enormous cake, three tiers high with the layers separated with crystal pillars and frosted in pink, with sparkles and a beautiful fairy on top. The villagers brought me presents, including a spotted pony, which the chieftain, George Yeoman, held on the greensward behind the mansion. I loved it!

"My mother swept through the kitchen dramatically, her long dress with its flared sleeves and hem sparkling with jewels, a maharajah's ransom of gems glittering on her throat, ears, fingers, and wrists. 'What is that mongrel doing on the rear lawn? George Yeoman, remove it, now!'

"Papa backed me up, for once, 'Ophelia, she's a child! A child is entitled ...'

"'Entitled to what? She has *everything* available to her, this entire estate, servants, clothes, and *food*; eventually she'll own *everything*. Unless I can conceive again, it all goes to *her*, that hideous, deformed, sniveling ...'"

"'Stop that, Ophelia! That's cruel, even for you!" He towered to his full height, peaked ruff suddenly standing up over his formal black and white dress. I saw his wand, very plain, old style, with a brilliant white tip.

"'What are you going to do, Heinrich, work a spell on me? The day you could do that is long gone.' Her glistening, white lace ruff protruded from the shadows of her neck. Her wand flashed in her hand, shooting sparks and mist along with sparkling letters that spelled her name as they floated to the floor. My mother had the gaudiest wand I've ever seen.

"'You're cruel to the child, woman.'

"'Cruel. I'll show you cruel.' She turned to the glass wall to the rear garden and swept her arm. My pony lay dead in the back yard, head severed from its neck. Mother spun, waving her wand at my beautiful cake. It melted into a pink puddle.

"I didn't think," Vanessa put her recorder down and took two solid swigs from the crystal glass before picking the dictation up once more. "My ruff shot from my bony, toddler neck. It's a severe, black *peau de soie* collar, quite tailored. Its protrusions were spiked, each spike ending in a jeweled tip, all black. Venom squirted ten feet. My wand was just *there*. Oversized, I've always liked an oversized ... *everything* ... Shiny black with diamond bands around the end. It blazed fire, sparks. *And anger.*

"I screamed, '*You are the worst parents in the world! I hate you! I curse you! You will change right now.*' I had no idea I was casting my first spell. 'You will become wonderful parents who are good and kind. You will never fight. You will be faithful to each other. You will take good care of me and treat the servants with respect. *You will become good!*'

"And then I fixed the cake and brought my pony back to life.

"It was that simple. 'How did you become a witch?' Stupid question. Witches are born, not made. It's not about spells and magic books. You have the Power, or you don't.

"From then on, my life was straightforward. My parents were transformed into good people. They raised me properly and saw that I had a good education. I'm a physicist, of course, with a PhD. I ask you not to forget that, however you distort what I give you, Sandy-writer-person." Vanessa shouted the last bit into the recorder.

"Enough. I'm going to bed."

A month later, Vanessa logged on to her computer. She had fed that author reams of stories about her life and felt exposed. Her life was a tragedy, and she'd told it all to some unknown writer who came into her life through a note on a bulletin board. True, she had a contract and could sue her to oblivion and bedevil her farther, but the pain of exposure. How could she bear it? "Invasive worm. Like a tropical parasite."

Vanessa checked the author's blog periodically to make sure she didn't publish anything about *her*. Her eyes widened. The title of the latest post read: How Did You Become a Witch?

There, in plain English, was all she'd told the tramp. At least the author-sow was kind enough to say she'd met a real witch and this is what *she* said. "She didn't claim it as *her* life …," Vanessa croaked. And she didn't mention Vanessa's name or the location of the estate.

"But she did not have my permission to publish this in her retched little blog or *anywhere!*"

Her ruff deployed, acid venom rising. Her wand, even larger now that she was a grown woman, shot fire and missiles of light.

Vanessa grabbed her iPhone, which she now used expertly. That was the one thing the author/worm had taught her. They were much more useful than ordinary people knew. She could push a button and reach the person on the other line, *really* reach them, by the "short and curlies" as a construction worker had so colorfully put it.

Not only that, Vanessa could touch everyone in the offender's social "network," including everyone connected to them through the iPhone and every other electronic web.

"NSA would love to know what I can do, and how."

But Vanessa would never tell. She clutched the iPhone, intending to cast a spell that would keep the author-creature from remembering her own name, much less writing anything. But what was that below the travesty of a blog post?

Comments. Many of them, 397, to be exact. She began reading them.

downycheeks: This is bullshit. This author is a lying scum who buys all her reviews. She steals the ideas for her books, too.

wanna****U: It's true. KittyKat did a report on her. Bitch is a total sleaze.

Whammomama: She doesn't deserve to live. I Googled her house. We can get you, author-bitch. You're stupid enough to use your real name.

Wombmanna: You're such a troll, Whammomama. *You* don't deserve to live. *I know where* you *live!*

A resounding chorus of bloodthirsty howls existing only as pixels followed. They had been ready to mount an attack on the offending author. This was not unfair: Vanessa thought she deserved *something* for spilling confidential material, but she was thinking of a nice law suit followed by sojourn in the lowest level of the basement beneath her home. Some quiet time to think about loyalty and the cost of betraying confidences. But not death!

Vanessa closed her eyes and increased the dense fog that wrapped everything about her life. She also created a little shield around the author. The faithless tramp didn't deserve it, but needed it. Google would no longer reveal or map her address. Hopefully, legitimate dinner guests would be able to find her place, but no one else.

Vanessa reloaded the blog page. The comment count was up to 821. She realized the individuals with the repulsive screen names were Internet trolls. The author had said she would run into them if she were on-line for any period of time. She said that clinical psychologists had done a study showing their personalities tested in "the dark triad" of the psychological world; they were heavy in narcissism, psychopathology, and sadism. They had no empathy for others and could harm them without remorse.

The modern cyber-world empowered *really* nasty people. They demonstrated their diagnoses with what they said about *The Author*, as well as what they said about *each other*. Real witches would never be so rude.

In a few comments, the on-line mob was threatening to attack their fellow blog interpreters. They knew each other very well, as the comments showed.

verminesque: You'll never change, bitchwad. I'm going to kill you. I should have killed you after what you said on die-a-ree-az's blog.

At about comment 121, they started attacking *her*, *Vanessa Schierman PhD*. They said *she* was a fake and liar, even though they didn't know her name and knew nothing about her. Or even if she really existed.

realwitch: The Author sez she's talking to a real witch. That's not a real witch. Only idiots would believe her shit and lies. Yer all idiots and don' deserve to live.

wawababy: realwitch is right: Real witches are tough. They aren't weenie cry-babies boo-hooin' cuz ther kids er sick.

On and on.

stubitch: Fake witch, I'm gonna carve yer eyes out. I know where you live.

Stupidbitchwitch summed it up with "You are a fountain of deceit, lies, and perfidy. You don't deserve to live."

Vanessa felt those were strong words from someone who had had no contact with her whatsoever. The language of the "discussion" steadily deteriorated.

humpmama: If yur such a f***in' witch, show us some Magick, you
******

Vanessa couldn't repeat the language when they began to demand she do some magic to show she was real. Didn't these trolls have any rules of decorum? Or spelling? She rebooted her computer. The blog now had close to two thousand comments, people vying with one another to be vicious and insulting.

She kept up with the discussion through the night. The post was reblogged and shared dozens of time. Twitter exploded with rage over the false witch.

"It's gone viral," Vanessa whispered.

One of the jeweled tips of her ruff squirted venom on her keyboard. It smoked, calling her attention to one of the more recent comments.

cumquat: You better show us some witching or we'll get you. Show us a monster or we'll get you and your children!

She had to stop the madness. Vanessa raised her hands and closed her eyes, incanting. Her energy, her thoughts, and her soul went into her computer and through it to the Internet around the world. And into everyone who had maligned her or thought of maligning her or *anyone*.

One thing she could not tolerate was bad manners. Also bad spelling. As she wove her incantation, the spelling and grammar of every nasty comment or note recorded anywhere instantly became correct. Swear words were transformed into appropriate, descriptive language and user names reflected the users' true character.

"Take that!" she shouted raising her hands and wand. She completed her magic with a few ancient phrases, best unrecorded.

The hall shook and the bats emerged prematurely into the light of dawn. The carvings on the wall ran frantically, craven creatures chasing each other, and being chased in return. The room throbbed.

Vanessa smiled. Every troll that lurked on the Internet or anywhere, waiting to bait and lie, waiting to hurt and distort and create malice and strife received the curse. One of her best and most powerful.

A bat alighted on her shoulder. The witch stroked its fine pelt.

"What are you saying, my darling? You want to know about the spell I cast?" She chuckled. "Only those who are true monsters will feel it. One evil thought or nasty impulse and the curse will fall on them.

"Real monsters can't see what they are. Now, everyone will see them truly. *They* are the monsters they wanted me to show them, darling."

Vanessa smiled, thinking, Dorian Gray, your time has run out.

Priscilla Porcine looked over her latest blog entry before posting it. Pris had tried writing books and found it tedious, hard work. Plus, her books didn't sell and got nasty reviews. Being an author was painful and too much work.

But writing about bad authors! Her natural talents as a sleuth leapt into play as her life's mission became apparent: Priscilla was on this earth to clean up the Internet. So many reviews were false, the results of friends and family boosting sales and rankings. Filthy, deceitful, lying *authors* bought reviews. They voted up *each other's* books.

She gave corrupt writers and false reviewers what they deserved. Acting as an investigative reporter, Pris found out the truth behind authors' apparently valid "platforms." She could see lies and deceit where no one else would.

For instance, the subject of her current exposé—and she outed about a hundred fraudulant authors a year—wrote romances about poodles. She had a dozen books in print, all highly ranked. That was first sign that something was wrong. No one could be that good.

Priscilla found scores of wondrous reviews and glowing testimonials about the fraudulant author's work. She had won a bunch of awards for independent authors, another sign of nefarious conduct. Those contests were rigged. The judges were paid off, and they didn't read the books anyway. They were part of a corrupt system.

As she delved into the woman's life, she discovered that something stank. It took weeks of investigation and hours of work to put it all together, but the proof existed in the duplicitous coward's personal blog. Of her writing ability, her target once said, "Writing about knitting is all I can do." She said that in 1989 in her blog for knitters.

That was definitive proof that the woman was not a true author! That it was published decades ago in a defunct hobby blog, Priscilla did not bother to report. Nor did she bother to mention the awards and all the good reviews.

Priscilla wrote of the woman in terms so damning, the devil wouldn't let her into hell. Would her friends love this one! Her followers would dump one star reviews by the dozens wherever she said. And Priscilla said: get this bitch!

She hit the publish button on her WordPress screen, noticing that her shoulder didn't seem to move right. Also, her fingers were separated, the pinky and ring fingers sticking together while the middle and index fingers adhered to her thumb. They were becoming hard, like horn.

As she watched, the sleeves of her blouse split, revealing her creamy white skin beneath the fabric. But it was thickened, like leather. Coarse black hair poked out of it. And rolls of fat piled up under the skin.

Priscilla jumped up, holding her hands in front of her. They were hooves! Cloven hooves. She hit the phone button on her keyboard. It took her a couple of shots; the hooves were hard to aim. Using the programmed number, she called her best friend and co-blogger, Sally Swiftblade.

When she answered, all Pris could do was make grunting noises. Like a pig. She put her hooves to her face, seeing if anything felt wrong. Tusks stuck out of her mouth on each side, sharp, deadly tusks.

"HEEE-HAW! HEE-HAW-haw-a-haw-a haw," came from the speaker. Was that Sally? Donkeys made that sound. What had happened? Pris tried to answer, but the grunting noises were all that came out.

Priscilla ran to her bathroom, having to drop to all fours to do it. Balancing on her rear hooves was impossible. Clattering and sliding on the hardwood floor, she clambered up on the toilet to see the mirror.

"AHHHHHHHH!"

"Now everyone will see them truly."
~ Vanessa Schierman

Illustration: Lily Nathan

FROM & ABOUT SANDY NATHAN

I hope you enjoy *Vanessa Schierman PhD WITCH*. Vanessa has appeared in my other books, particularly *In Love by Christmas,* but she's never had a starring role. Wendy Potocki's Halloweenpalooza motivated me to give Vanessa her due. Wendy's Halloween-themed on-line festival for authors and readers of the macabre is unique. I love the sheer wackiness of Halloween and applaud Wendy for creating an event around it.

In this book, I introduce you to a special woman, who is entirely fictional, and entirely based on a woman I knew. Her estate and world are parts of my youth. Only a veil of imagination separates what I experienced as a child from the dark mansion on the mountain in this tale.

I was born to be a princess. I *was* a princess, for a while. My parents overcame the poverty of their youth by becoming extremely successful. My hometown was one of the most affluent places in the country. Giant oaks, old mansions, and flashy cars surrounded me. I spent my time showing horses and water-skiing behind my dad's obscenely overpowered boat.

"The Schierman estate" really exists. I discovered it while riding my horse through the redwoods of the coastal range in the San Francisco Peninsula around 1960. I was totally lost—fences were rare in those days—I rode around a bend in the tall trees and ferns and found myself confronted by a magnificent, historic mansion. Acres of emerald lawns and glorious evergreens ringed the ancient structure. I've never forgotten that breathless moment. The grand house I found wasn't scary; it was beautiful and surprising and truly magical. The one in my story was designed to terrify anyone who saw it.

Dr. Vanessa Schierman is based on a real person, a very tall, gaunt, and extremely wealthy woman with exquisite manners and enough kindness and love to stock the planet. She wasn't a witch, but she embodied Dr. Schierman's ideas about taste and decorum. And she was a direct descendent of a Robber Baron. Her family's bloodlines and influence reached far into the past. She defines a truly upper class person to me.

My life as a princess ended when a drunk driver ran into my father head-on in 1964, killing him. Not instantaneously, either. My dad's death was the stuff of horror movies.

My old life vanished. All the horses, water-ski boats, and parties went Poof! Through structures and systems I will not describe, I lived at a close to poverty level income for a while. What happened in the coming years opened my eyes. I've seen and lived the over-privileged existence I describe in my novels. I've seen how ephemeral its rewards are and how it warps those who are trapped by it. I've seen how it masks mental illness.

My writing has a bite. My life has had a bite. Recovering from what happened to me has taken many years. And I have recovered. What was legitimately mine came back to me, along with the fruit of my own labor. If your life echoes mine, you might like to see how I healed; it's in my books. I write fiction so that I can tell the truth without being sued.

Now for my "regular bio": I've been in school a very long time and have two advanced degrees. I've had prestigious careers. My writing has won thirty national awards and I am an Amazon bestselling author in a number of categories. I'm very happily married; my husband and I have been together forty-two years. I have three grown children and two grandchildren. We live on our California horse ranch.

ALSO BY SANDY NATHAN

FICTION

THE BLOODSONG SERIES
Numenon: A Tale of Mysticism & Money (Bloodsong 1)
Mogollon: A Tale of Mysticism & Mayhem (Bloodsong 2)
Leroy Watches Jr. & the Badass Bull (A Bloodsong Novella)
In Love by Christmas: A Paranormal Romance (Bloodsong 4)

BLOODSONG SERIES, UNNUMBERED:
MINDSPEAK/HEARTSPEAK:
A Tale of Quantum Physics, Alternative Universes & Love
Vanessa Schierman PhD: WITCH

EARTH'S END TRILOGY
The Angel & the Brown-Eyed Boy (Earth's End 1)
Lady Grace & the War for a New World (Earth's End 2)
The Headman & the Assassin (Earth's End 3)
The Earth's End Trilogy (Earth's End 1 to 3 in a single eBook)

NONFICTION & CHILDREN'S LITERATURE

Stepping Off the Edge: A Roadmap for the Soul
Tecolote: The Little Horse That Could

Reviews are very important in determining books' rankings.

If you'd like to review Sandy Nathan's books,
you can find them on Sandy's Author Page:
http://www.amazon.com/Sandy-Nathan/e/B001JS6VMI/

Sign up for Sandy's Readers' Club on her website. You'll be the first to know about new books or works. You'll get free downloads and other goodies you can't get anywhere else.
http://sandynathan.com/